Match Wits with The Hardy Boys®!

Collect the Original
Hardy Boys Mystery Stories®
by Franklin W. Dixon

Celebrate 60 Years with the World's Greatest Super Sleuths!

THE MELTED COINS

FRANK and Joe Hardy suspect that their best friend Chet Morton is the victim of a summer school swindle and offer to help get his money back. While probing a baffling burglary at the Seneca Indian Reservation in New York State they investigate Zoar College located nearby.

Clues that Frank and Joe uncover indicate that there is a connection between the Zoar College swindle and the theft of the Senecas' gold tribal relic Spoon Mouth. This startling discovery propels the teen-age sleuths into a series of perplexing and dangerous situations.

Two strange-acting college professors, a valuable coin collection, and a taciturn Indian who refuses to discuss the mystery surrounding Spoon Mouth—all blend into a fast-paced story with several surprise twists that will thrill the vast legion of Hardy boys' fans.

Joe hung on tight

The Hardy Boys Mystery Stories®

THE
MELTED
COINS

BY

FRANKLIN W. DIXON

GROSSET & DUNLAP
Publishers • New York
A member of The Putnam & Grosset Group

Printed on Recycled Paper

CONTENTS

THE
MELTED
COINS

CHAPTER I

Highway Trouble

CHET Morton strode about the Hardys' living room, waving a white booklet. "I tell you, fellows, I'll be a college man in just a few months!"

Joe Hardy, blond-haired and seventeen, looked skeptical. "A six-week summer course at Zoar College in New York State will get you a full year's credit?"

"Of course. It says so right here."

Joe's brother Frank, dark-haired and a year older, took the brochure and scanned it. "Listen, Chet. I wouldn't pay more than the twenty-five dollars' application fee until I saw the place!"

Just then his father entered. Fenton Hardy, an internationally famous detective, was a tall, athletic-looking man.

"Did I hear you mention Zoar Valley?" he asked. "If you're going there, how about doing some sleuthing for me?"

Joe grinned. "Any time, Dad. What's it all about?"

Mr. Hardy seated himself in an armchair. "It has something to do with the Indians at the Seneca Reservation near Zoar Valley. Rod Jimerson, a Seneca who lives in Cleveland, phoned me recently asking me to take a case for him. It involves somebody known as Spoon Mouth."

"Spoon Mouth?" Chet said. "Reminds me of food." He called to the boys' aunt as she passed the kitchen door. "Oh, Aunt Gertrude, could you make me a cream cheese and salami sandwich?"

"Here we go again!" Joe ribbed their roly-poly buddy, who would rather eat than sleuth. "I suppose you want the salami lean and the crust trimmed from the bread."

"What else?" Chet said breezily. He handed the Zoar College brochure to Frank and lumbered into the kitchen.

Mr. Hardy's peppery spinster sister disapproved of the detective work in which her nephews were constantly involved. She scolded them often for getting themselves into dangerous situations, but her affection showed through, especially when it came to cooking up a tasty dish.

With a deftness born of long practice, she now whipped a sandwich onto the kitchen table and placed a tall glass of milk beside it. Chet made short work of the treat, then rejoined Frank, Joe, and their father, who was studying the catalog.

"I think you'd better check up on this college, Chet," Mr. Hardy said. "It seems like a very small faculty."

"That's right, sir. I figured that it's pretty exclusive. Only the best professors."

"Or else the leftovers," Frank said.

"Well, you've got a few weeks before it opens," the detective said. "It might not be a bad idea to drive out there and look the place over."

"That's right," Joe said. "And if we find Spoon Mouth, we'll see if he has a bigger appetite than Chet!"

Mr. Hardy said that he hoped he was not sending them on a wild-goose chase. "I'd go myself," he declared, "but I'm working on a mail fraud case and can't get away." He added that the call from Rod Timerson had been garbled. "The connection was bad, and finally we were cut off. But I have his address in Cleveland."

"Hey, I have an idea!" Chet spoke up. "You know, I sent my application to the Zoar College offices in Cleveland. Maybe we can kill two birds with one stone and check there first!"

"Good idea." Joe was enthusiastic. "When do we leave?"

"How about tomorrow?" Chet asked.

"Okay," Frank said. "Let's start about six in the morning. We can take the New York Thruway for a good part of the trip."

By the middle of the next morning, Bayport

had been left far behind. Chet lolled in the back seat. Frank was driving. Long before noon, Chet complained of a maddening hunger. The trio stopped for gasoline, hot dogs, and cold drinks. Then Joe spelled Frank at the wheel.

At an even speed they passed through the beautiful rolling country of New York State. The highway divider was sometimes a meadow, sometimes a craggy island of trees.

As Joe drove up a hill Chet called out, "Hey, look at that guy! He's having trouble!"

A quarter of a mile away, in the opposite lane, a car approached with front wheels wobbling. Joe slowed down and pulled onto the shoulder to watch the crippled vehicle.

Suddenly it swerved onto the center island and careened over the grass.

"Holy Toledo!" Joe said. "He's going to hit us!"

He gunned the motor, whipping up gravel as the convertible shot forward. The oncoming car missed them by inches, rolled into a ditch, and landed on its top, all four wheels spinning.

Joe set the emergency brake and the three boys jumped out and ran to the wreck. Inside they saw a man and woman, both elderly, struggling to get out. In the rear seat were two huge German shepherds.

"Good night! Look at those dogs! Chet said.

"He's going to hit us!" Joe cried out

He gingerly opened the rear door while Frank and Joe took care of the people in front. They were pulled out, dazed, but there was no sign of serious injury.

The dogs, too, looked befuddled. Chet found their leashes in the rear and snapped them onto the collars of the groggy beasts.

"Better sit down on the grass," Frank said to the couple as he and Joe eased them onto the ground. Chet tethered the dogs to the door handle, then examined the front wheels, which by now had stopped spinning.

"Your steering is shot!" he said. "How did it happen?"

The man smiled wanly. "I don't know. All of a sudden I couldn't control the car and tried to push the brake."

"I think you must have gotten excited and hit the gas instead," Joe said, "the way you shot across the median strip."

The woman spoke for the first time. Her hands were shaking as a result of the shock. "They've been calling back a lot of cars recently. Maybe this is one of the faulty ones."

"Well, your garage mechanic will find out soon enough," Frank said. "Do you live around here?"

"No, we live in Hawk Head," the man replied. "I'm Dr. Rideau and this is my wife."

As the boys introduced themselves, cars driving by were slowing down to rubberneck at the wreck and soon a State Police car pulled up. Frank told what they had seen and added, "It was a miraculous escape, Officer. They seem to be okay."

"We can't take chances," the policeman replied. "I'll get an ambulance." He walked to his car and radioed for help.

Frank, Joe, and Chet gave their names as witnesses to the accident, then said good-by to the Rideaus.

"I'm a retired dentist," the man said, shaking Joe's hand. "You have been very kind to us. If you should find yourself in our area, please drop in to see us. Remember—Hawk Head, New York."

"You must come for dinner," Mrs. Rideau added.

Chet beamed. "You bet we will. Thanks for the invitation."

The boys proceeded without further incident the rest of the day. It was night before they reached Cleveland, and they found a comfortable motel at the edge of the city. Tired from the long trip, they went to bed right after dinner.

"We'll look up Rod Jimerson first thing in the morning," Frank said.

"Wait a minute," Chet pleaded. "Since you're so suspicious of Zoar College, why don't we go there first? If it's a phony, I want my twenty-five dollars back."

"I thought you were convinced it was a great college," Joe reminded him.

"Well, you never—can—tell." Chet's lips puffed a couple of times, then he dropped off into a gentle snore.

As they finished breakfast the next morning, Frank reconsidered their plans. "Okay, Chet, we'll take your advice and go to the Zoar office first," he said.

With Frank at the wheel, they drove into downtown Cleveland. Joe studied the map and directed his brother. They passed the tall new buildings, drove into a side street, and continued into an older part of the city.

"Good night, is it down here?" asked Chet.

Glancing up at a row of dilapidated buildings, he spied the faded number on a dirty glass door. Frank parked the car in the next open spot. He locked it and the trio walked back.

"There must be some mistake," Chet mumbled.

"Well, you said it was exclusive," Joe needled.

They took a rickety self-service elevator to the third floor, walked down a hall, and came to a door marked Z.C.

Stepping inside, they found themselves in a dingy office. To the left was a switchboard, presided over by a stout blond girl who chewed gum furiously. She pulled out a plug and adjusted her headset. Then she swung around in her chair and stared at the visitors. "Yes, please?"

"We'd like to speak to somebody from Zoar College," Chet spoke up.

The switchboard buzzed, and the girl turned around, inserting a jack. "Yes, this is the Bondway Trucking Company. . . . No, there's nobody in. . . . Will you leave a message?"

She jotted down something on a pad, pulled the plug, and looked at the boys.

"We must be in the wrong office," Frank said.

"No you're not," the girl said matter-of-factly.

"We don't want a trucking company," Joe informed her.

"I answer the phone for them. They have desk space here," she replied tartly.

Just then a door opened and a thin youth who looked about nineteen drifted into the office. He had a sallow face and huge eyes partly covered by a mop of hair.

The girl nodded toward him. "They're looking for Zoar College," she said.

"What do you want?" the youth asked coldly.

Chet blurted, "I paid my twenty-five bucks and I want to be sure—"

The boy looked him up and down slowly. "Take down his address and phone number, Mabel."

Frank brought out a matchbook he had taken from their motel which bore the address and number.

"Room fifteen," he said.

"We'll be in touch with you," the woman said.

The boys left. As they walked down the windy street, Frank glanced over his shoulder and noticed the youth behind them. Then a gust blew up and he had to squint to keep dust from getting into his eyes.

"What do you make of that high-class establishment?" Joe asked Frank.

"Think it's a phony?" Chet queried.

Frank shrugged. "Wait till they call us. We'll probably find out then."

"Where to now?" Joe asked.

"We'll go see Dad's client."

Frank consulted a street map for the address their father had given them. It was clear across town in a residential section. They found the house, parked, and walked up to the door.

A woman answered the bell. She said that Rod Jimerson had a room there but was at work.

"Do you mind telling us where?" Frank asked.

"Not at all. He's an ironworker on one of the new office buildings going up downtown." She gave directions and the boys thanked her.

On the way to the car, Joe happened to glance back. "Hey, isn't that the creepy office boy from Zoar College?" he asked.

"Looks like him," Frank replied.

The youth was slumped behind the wheel of a fairly new car parked some distance behind them.

"Why is he tailing us?" Chet wondered nervously.

"Maybe he wants to return your twenty-five bucks," Joe quipped.

"He doesn't strike me as the charitable type," Frank said. "I don't like this."

After turning several corners they managed to lose the trailing car. Soon they came to the construction site. Frank had to drive around the block three times before finding a suitable parking spot.

The building loomed above them like a giant skeleton, its bare steel beams towering skyward. On the street was a freight elevator. Beside it was a stack of hardhats used by the construction men.

"Where can we find Rod Jimerson?" Joe asked a man who was loading brick onto the elevator.

"He's up with the angels, right on top."

"Mind if we join you?"

"Hop aboard if it's important."

"It sure is."

The elevator rattled to the top, where the boys stepped off onto a narrow platform. Construction workers were guiding a girder, which was being lowered by a boom.

"Hey, what are you doing here?" a workman demanded.

"Are you the foreman?" Frank asked.

"That's me."

"We'd like to speak to Rod Jimerson."

"Who gave you permission to come up here?"

"Nobody," Joe said. "But we'd like to see Jimerson for a moment. It's important."

"Okay, he's over there. But be careful!" The foreman pointed to a young man tightening a bolt with a large wrench.

Joe stepped toward him, balancing on top of a high beam. He looked down, then quickly averted his eyes from the long drop.

He had moved only a few steps when a blast of wind whipped across the top of the framework. Joe teetered, lost his balance, and plunged!

CHAPTER II

Motel Knockout

JOE dropped with arms outstretched, wrists bent and fingers clawed like grappling hooks. He touched the edge of the girder and hung on tight.

Shouts went up all around him but he heard them only faintly as his body swayed in the stiff wind. His knuckles grew white. The strength seemed to be draining out of his aching arms.

"Hold it, I'll get you!" Rod Jimerson called out. He put his tool aside and worked his way along the girder. Leaning over, he grasped Joe's wrists in his viselike hands, then hoisted the exhausted boy up beside him.

"Easy now," he said, and guided Joe back along the girder to the platform where Frank and Chet stood, white-faced but vastly relieved.

"Thank you," Joe managed to say weakly. "Boy, I thought my number was up!"

"We almost had to pick you up in pieces," Frank said.

"That was a careless thing to do," the foreman yelled angrily at Joe.

Rod Jimerson held up his hand. "Hold it, Mike! He's had enough. I don't think he realized how dangerous it was."

The foreman mopped his head. "I know, I know. But I'm responsible up here and an accident is all I need!" Shaking his head, he walked away.

"We came to see you, Mr. Jimerson," Frank spoke up.

"You did?" The Seneca's eyebrows lifted and his tanned forehead wrinkled above his high cheekbones. "Well, let's go down to the street where we can talk."

After the freight elevator had rattled to the bottom of the steel frame, all four stepped out onto the wooden sidewalk and stood in the shade of a gallery which protected pedestrians.

"Now, what's it all about?" Rod Jimerson asked.

Frank quickly told him the story and added, "It seems you had a bad phone connection, Mr. Jimerson. But why didn't you call Dad back later?"

"I did, but the line was busy. Then other things came up."

"Well," Joe said, who by now had recovered from his shock, "we're here to help you if we can."

"What about this person called Spoon Mouth?" Frank put in. "Is he lost or did he run away?"

Rod Jimerson laughed, tilted back his hardhat, and said, "Spoon Mouth is not a person." He explained that Spoon Mouth was a highly revered object which had been stolen from the Indians.

"Something like an idol, you mean?" Chet asked.

"No, I wouldn't say that. There's a lot to tell, but I've got to get back to work." He glanced at his watch and added, "Where are you fellows staying? Maybe I could meet you tonight."

"Okay," Frank said, and gave the Indian their address. "I know you're not getting paid to bat the breeze, Mr. Jimerson."

"Rod."

"Good enough, Rod," Frank shook his hand. "Suppose we meet at the motel at nine."

"Suits me."

Frank watched the Seneca return to the elevator and press the buzzer. Soon he was soaring to the top of the steel skeleton.

"He looks like a real interesting guy," Chet remarked as they returned to the car.

"And is he strong!" Joe added. "He picked me up like a sack of potatoes."

They had just entered their room in the motel when the phone rang. Frank dashed for it and lifted the receiver. The voice at the other end was smooth and self-possessed. The man identified himself as Dr. John Snedecker, president of Zoar College.

"Then you want to speak to Chet Morton," Frank said. "He's right here, sir. Hold the wire."

Chet took the phone and smiled into the mouthpiece. "Hello, Dr. Snedecker."

There was silence for a few moments. "Oh, I knew there must have been a mistake. . . . You say I went to the wrong office? . . . Yes, sir. Hold on until I get the new number." Quickly he jotted it down on a pad next to the telephone.

There was more talk on the other end, then Chet said, "Suppose I bring my friends, Frank and Joe Hardy." A pause. "Okay, I'll be there."

"Now what was that all about?" Frank said after Chet had hung up.

"This call proves that I was right after all," Chet said with an air of injured dignity. He explained that Dr. Snedecker wanted him to come to their new offices. "I asked to take you along, but he said he was too busy to have anyone else in on the conversation."

"What do you think he'll tell you?" Joe asked as he flopped down on one of the beds.

"I don't know," Chet replied with a shrug. "Guess he just wants to interview his future star student."

"That'll be the day!" Frank said, poking Chet's massive rib cage. "When is your appointment, hotshot?"

"Right away, sooner if possible," Chet replied. He stood before the mirror, using the palms of his hands to smooth his hair which had been whipped by the wind.

"Where?"

Chet gave the name of the building and the room number.

"Look, Chet, I don't like the idea of your going there alone," Frank said. "Remember that creepy guy who followed us?"

"Don't worry. I can handle him."

Nonetheless the Hardys convinced their friend that they should at least accompany him to the place. They would then wait downstairs in the lobby while he had his interview.

The building was an outstanding steel-and-glass model of architectural beauty. The boys pushed through the front doors, walked into an impressive lobby, and escorted Chet to a bank of elevators.

"Take it easy now," Joe advised him. "And don't let any gorgeous secretaries turn your head."

"I'm perfectly immune to such charms," Chet said loftily. He stepped into an elevator, punched the number eight button, and a second later was gone.

Frank and Joe turned to wander about the vast lobby. "Maybe the college deal is not a phony after all," Joe said.

"Let's have a look at the directory board," Frank suggested.

They walked to a huge board listing the tenants who occupied the building. Frank looked under the Z column.

"Joe, they're not listed."

"Well, obviously they just moved here. Maybe they haven't been entered on the board yet."

"I have a hunch that Chet might be in trouble. Let's go after him!"

They went across the hall and saw one of the elevators yawn open. Quickly they stepped inside, pushed the number eight button, and started upward.

Alighting at the eighth floor, Frank and Joe looked left and right, then did a double-take as Chet approached them with a lively spring in his gait. His round face was beaming.

"Is everything all right?" Joe asked.

"Certainly," Chet replied. "As a matter of fact, it sounds just beautiful!" He reported that Dr. Snedecker had been extremely cordial. "He even offered to return my money if I had any doubts about his college."

"Did you take it?"

"Of course not. I refused. With offices like those, old Snedecker must be worth a million!"

"I still don't like the whole thing," Frank said, glancing uneasily at Joe. "You and Chet go on down. I'm going to check out this Suite 825."

"But, Frank—" Chet started to protest.

Joe steered him to the elevator. "Come on. Big boss knows what he's doing."

Frank walked down the hall, found the number, and stepped into a small vestibule. It was tastefully decorated with a Louis XIV chair, small marble-top table, and a vase filled with artificial flowers. An inner door was marked with gilded letters, but they did not announce Zoar College. Instead, they spelled out *Magnitude Merchandising Mart*.

Frank opened the door and stepped inside. A smiling, attractive dark-haired receptionist, smartly dressed, sat behind a desk. Several doors led into cubicle offices.

"May I help you?" the girl asked.

"Yes," Frank replied. His eyes roved about and he leaned first on one foot, then the other, feigning embarrassment.

"Well, what is it?" the girl went on.

"I guess I have the wrong place," Frank said. "I'm looking for Zoar College."

The receptionist smiled even more sweetly and flicked a wisp of raven hair back in place. "Yes, I'm afraid you do," she said.

"Well, is there a Dr. Snedecker here?" Frank asked, still gawking about.

"Look, young man, this is not a doctor's office. I must ask you to leave."

"No offense," Frank said. "Thank you, miss."

He backed out of the office, returned to the elevator, and joined the others in the lobby.

"Hi, wasn't that brunette a doll?" Chet asked.

"I thought you weren't susceptible to female charms," Frank replied.

"She's Snedecker's secretary," Chet went on, ignoring the gibe. "Took me right into his office. Brand-new place, you know. They just moved in. Didn't have time to put the name on the door yet."

"That's strange. Your doll didn't even know Snedecker when I asked for him," Frank replied.

Chet's eyebrows went up. "Oh? Well, perhaps you're talking about a different girl."

Frank did not pursue the matter. "How about chauffeuring us back, Chet?"

"Sure thing." Chet walked on ahead while Frank quickly briefed his brother.

"Wow, what a hoax!" Joe said. "How can poor Chet be so naive?"

Frank shrugged. "Maybe that brunette blinded him to the harsh facts of life!"

Chet drove carefully, threading his way through the heavy traffic in the downtown streets. He pulled up in front of their motel room, jumped out of the car, and opened the door for Frank and Joe with a smart salute.

Frank went along with the game. "Thank you, James," he said with a grin.

Joe inserted the key in the lock. When he opened the door, all three gasped at what they saw. The place had been ransacked! Their suitcases lay open, and their clothes were strewn about. Frank reached over to pull a T-shirt from the top of a mirror.

"Somebody's trying to give us the old one-two," Joe said in disgust. He held up a pair of slacks with the legs cut to shreds.

"And my new jacket!" Chet moaned. It had been slashed beyond repair.

"Okay, fellows. Let's report this," Frank said, his voice shaking with anger. They hastened to the motel office and told the manager, who called the police.

An officer arrived within a few minutes and looked over the situation.

"Nothing is missing," Joe said. "But a lot of things are damaged."

The policeman shook his head. "There has been a lot of vandalism in the area," he said. "This is terrible!"

"But why would anyone do this to us?" Chet asked.

The officer shrugged. "We'll keep a watch on this place. If we find out anything, we'll let you know."

The boys began to straighten up the room after he had left. "I don't think this is just an ordinary case of vandalism," Frank said thoughtfully. "I have a hunch somebody around here doesn't care for us and did this to get rid of us."

"Maybe Dr. Snedecker didn't like your poking your nose into his office, Frank," Joe suggested.

"But that's ridiculous!" Chet protested.

"Calm down, Chet," Frank said. "You know we can't overlook any possibility."

"How about something to eat?" Joe asked. "I'm getting hungry."

"That's for me!" Chet perked up, and the three went out to dinner.

When they returned to the motel they discussed the strange events again. Presently they heard someone walking up to their door. Before they had a chance to see who it was, there was a gasp and a thud.

Frank jumped up and opened the door. A man lay on the welcome mat, unconscious.

Rod Jimerson!

CHAPTER III

The False Face Society

FRANK and Joe leaned down to pick up the fallen man. Putting his arms over their shoulders, they carried him into their room and placed him on a bed.

Chet dashed into the bathroom to soak a washcloth with cold water. When he put it against Jimerson's face, the Indian shook his head, blinked, and slowly sat up.

"Somebody bushwhacked you," Frank told him.

Jimerson winced and put a hand to the back of his head. "You're not kidding!" He got up and made his way to a chair. Chet and Frank sat on the beds, while Joe pulled over a hassock.

"Rod, do you have any enemies?" Frank asked. "Somebody who'd want to bop you on the head like that?"

"None at all," Jimerson replied. He squinted as

if searching his memory. "I can't think of anybody. How about you fellows? Maybe someone was after you!"

Frank shrugged. "Our room was vandalized while we were out. It's quite possible that you were mistaken for one of us."

The ironworker snapped his fingers. "Wait a minute. There is one man I don't like—or rather, I think, he doesn't like me!"

"Who is it?" Joe inquired.

"Lendo Wallace. He's an Indian from the reservation. We're both members of the False Face Society."

The boys looked confused, so Rod explained that some of the Senecas still believed in their old religion. "The society is part of it," he said. "The false faces represent spirits. In the spring and the fall we go through the homes in our community wearing them to drive out evil spirits."

"Sounds eerie," Chet remarked.

Rod grinned and went on, "Some of the false faces are medicine masks and have powers to cure diseases. They're blocked out on a living tree, then the chunk is cut away and the carving finished elsewhere."

"Must be hard on the tree," Joe said.

"The carver takes care of that all right," Jimerson went on. "First, the tree is placated by burning tobacco leaves beneath it. We wave the smoke high up in the branches and the tree understands that the carving is for a good purpose." He smiled. "Most of them heal."

"But what about Lendo Wallace?" Frank pressed. "What has he got against you?"

Rod said that in the past year, rare and valuable medicine masks, some of them very old, had been disappearing from the homes of various members of the tribe.

"Our longhouse was even raided once and some of the ancient false faces taken," he remarked.

"What's the longhouse?" Chet asked.

"Our community building, where we meet for ceremonies and dances." Rod frowned. "Without the medicine faces, we can't hold our ceremonies."

"How does Wallace fit into all this?" asked Joe.

"He's the leader of the False Face Society. Some of us think he ought to be more concerned about these thefts, and I've told him so. I'm afraid he didn't like that."

Jimerson rubbed his chin thoughtfully and added, "He doesn't seem to worry about the thefts. Maybe he's possessed by an evil spirit himself, because all this happened after Spoon Mouth was stolen."

"This case seems to be even more complicated than we at first thought," Frank said. "Spoon Mouth was stolen, you said?"

"I know it's confusing to an outsider," Rod said. "Just be patient; I'll explain."

As the three listened intently, he told them that Spoon Mouth was a flat golden replica of a Spoon Mouth false face. Taking a pencil and a pad which lay beside the telephone, he drew a queer-looking face, with a mouth like a figure eight lying on its side.

Joe chuckled. "That boy is well-named. Each end of his mouth is round as a spoon!"

"Right. With his protruding lips he's quite a scary sight," Rod said. "He was found by my tribe during the French and Indian Wars."

"When was that?" Chet remarked, scratching his head.

"They went on for seventy-four years until 1763. The relic was found near the end. Some of the tribe believed it to be a protector of the Five Nations."

"You lost me again," Chet said.

Rod smiled. "There used to be Five Nations in the Iroquois federation. The Senecas were one of them. Later there were six. My ancestors thought the relic had been blessed by Orinda, the Life Spirit, because after its discovery the Indians were extremely successful in battle."

"I don't know much about the Iroquois," Joe said.

"That's right," Frank agreed. "Mostly we hear about the Western Indians."

"There are still plenty of us in the East," Rod

said. He added that many of his tribe were employed as ironworkers, both in Cleveland and New York City.

"That's probably because you're so fearless," Chet said.

Jimerson smiled. "Oh, I wouldn't say we're fearless. But some of us don't mind heights."

"Did you want my father to find out who stole the false faces?" Frank spoke up.

"Yes. They are tremendously important to our tribe."

"Well, he's on another case, but he sent us to look into this matter. And I think we should start out by learning more about this fellow Lendo Wallace and the False Face Society."

Rod referred the boys to his mother, who lived on the Yellow Springs Reservation. "She knows all about everybody," he said. "Perhaps my kid brother is there, too. He's been working in Buffalo lately."

"Okay, Rod. We'll go there tomorrow," Frank promised.

"Good. Once we get Spoon Mouth back, I think things will go much better with the tribe," Rod said. Looking directly at Chet, he added, "If you see my mother, ask for her specialty, corn soup."

Chet grinned. "How did you know I like to eat?"

"Just guessed." Rod then mentioned a fee for

the boys' sleuthing services, but Frank waved him off. "Don't worry about that now," he said.

"Okay, fellows, I'll be seeing you." Rod gave each a finger-crushing handshake and departed.

In mock horror, Chet pried one finger from the other. "That guy thinks he's holding a wrench," he complained. "Well, when are we leaving?"

Joe suggested the next morning and added, "It's not far from Hawk Head. Perhaps we can stop and say hello to the Rideaus."

"Good thought. They invited us for dinner!"

The next day when the boys were checking out of the motel, the manager said, "I have a letter for Chet Morton."

Looking pleased, the stout boy took the envelope and opened it. As he studied the letter, his chin fell. "From Zoar College," he said and read it to the Hardys:

" 'Dear Mr. Morton: On checking your credentials we find that you are ineligible for the Zoar College summer course.' "

Enclosed with the note was Chet's money. "What a rotten trick!" he grumbled. "What do you make of this?"

"I told you before I thought the whole thing was fishy," Frank replied. "Anyway, you got your money back."

"It's strange that they sent it in cash," Joe remarked. "Let's go see this Zoar College when we get upstate New York."

"Okay. Before we leave, I think we ought to call home," Frank said.

While Joe paid the bill, he put in a call to his father, giving him a quick rundown on what had happened. When Mr. Hardy heard the name Magnitude Merchandising Mart he let out a low whistle.

"What's the matter, Dad? Do you know that outfit?" Frank asked.

"I've heard about it and it bears some investigating."

"Connected with your mail fraud case?"

"Yes, Frank. But keep it under your hat for the time being at least. You fellows may have handed me a good lead."

The detective wished his sons luck in the Spoon Mouth case, but warned them to be careful. "I suggest you leave Cleveland immediately," he concluded.

"We intend to, Dad. In fact we're on our way now," Frank told him and hung up.

Ten minutes later they were rolling along the highway out of Cleveland, enjoying the morning sunshine. Chet luxuriated in the back seat, taking in the beauty of the countryside. He happened to glance behind him.

"Oh, no!" he moaned. "There's Creepy again!"

"The office boy? Are you sure?" Frank asked, looking into the rear-view mirror.

He slowed down and the trailing car did likewise. The cat-and-mouse game lasted for miles. Then, slowed nearly to a stop by two passing trucks, Creepy tailgated, touching his front bumper to the rear of the convertible.

"Hope he doesn't play any hot-rod tricks," Joe said.

Chet turned around, shook his fist, and shouted, "Get off our backs, Creepy!"

With traffic flowing again, their pursuer poured on the gas, pushing the Hardys' car ahead. Frank knew this could easily throw them out of control. He accelerated, but still Creepy's car bore hard against the convertible.

As their back end slewed around, the pillar of an overpass loomed in front of them. Frank's expert driving prevented a head-on crash, but the convertible sideswiped the concrete and came to a grinding halt.

Creepy's car flashed by and was lost in the traffic ahead. Moments later a police car, siren wailing, drove up and stopped. The officer was polite but firm. After examining Frank's license, he said, "Looks as if you fellows were hot-rodding along here."

"We weren't," Frank protested, and told what had happened.

"One of your buddies playing footsy with you?" the officer asked.

"He wasn't our buddy!" Joe said hotly.

The officer half smiled, indicating he did not

believe their story. He proceeded to write out a summons.

"Here," he said, handing it to Frank. "The charge is careless driving. The judge will be receiving guests tonight between eight and nine."

"You mean our whole day's shot?" Frank exclaimed. "We'll have to wait around?"

"I didn't make the rules," the policeman replied. While he held up traffic, Frank started the car. It groaned and scratched as it finally cleared the abutment. The officer acted as escort while the damaged car crossed the median strip and pulled into the opposite flow of traffic.

Joe was furious. "Boy, just let me get my hands on that creepy character and he won't recognize himself when I'm through with him!"

"He sure got us into a first-class jam," Frank agreed. "And obviously for a reason."

"I can't figure it out," Chet put in. "If he wanted to get rid of us, why didn't he just let us go? We were leaving Cleveland."

"He probably figured we'd go upstate and have a look at the college," Frank said. "And they've got something to hide!"

For the rest of the day the boys went from one body shop to another, getting estimates on the repair work. They did not leave the car to be fixed, however.

"We'd better wait till tomorrow and see what happens in court tonight," Frank decided.

"That's right," Chet said glumly. "We might not even have enough money left to continue the trip."

At eight o'clock the boys reported to court and sat on a bench waiting for their turn. Fines were meted out to several drivers before their case came up.

The judge was a man in his middle thirties with a touch of gray at the temples and a severe mouth. He examined the summons, then reached for another piece of paper. After studying it, he said, "You Bayporters are really up to high jinks. Don't you know it's unsafe to cut in and out along the highway?"

"I don't know what you mean," Frank said.

"I have received no less than three complaints from motorists in this area today." He read Frank's license plate number. "That's you?"

"Yes, sir."

"These drivers," the judge went on, "said you were cutting in and out of traffic endangering their lives!"

"That's a lie!" Joe said hotly. "Somebody is trying to frame us!"

The judge frowned. Unimpressed by Joe's protest, he announced, "I sentence you to a fine of fifty dollars and three days in jail!"

CHAPTER IV

Treasure Below

"BUT that's not fair! You can't do this to my brother!" Joe declared. "He's innocent!"

"Silence!" the judge replied. "Something has to be done to make an example of young people using our highways to play games!"

"But, Your Honor, those complaints are faked!" said Frank. "Won't you please give us a chance for an investigation of our own?"

The judge studied the three boys for a moment, then said, "I'll give you four days of grace before you start to serve your sentence. You are not allowed to leave this area. Next case!"

Frank hurried to the nearest public telephone. With Joe and Chet crowding around him, he dialed their home in Bayport. No one was there.

"Try Radley," Joe advised. Sam Radley was Mr. Hardy's operative. He was home.

Frank explained his predicament and said,

"Sam, this is a real SOS. If I can't prove I was framed I'll be spending some time in the cooler."

"Okay. Where are you staying?"

"In the Ohio Motel. We stayed there before and I'm sure we'll get another room."

"I'll catch the next flight out and meet you there," Sam said.

Radley arrived at the motel early the next morning. "Good thing I was home," he said with a grin. "Your father's out of town on his mail fraud case. Now give me the details!"

Frank reported what had happened the night before, and Radley started to work at once. It did not take the experienced detective long to check out the complaints against Frank. One was from a man who had died the year before. Another man had moved and was a resident of California. The third complaint was fictitious.

When Sam met the boys for lunch in the motel coffee shop, he waved a piece of paper in his hand. "All right, you're off the hook. Here's your release, signed by the judge!"

The trio broke into relieved exclamations and questions.

"How'd you manage to get hold of the judge so fast?" Frank asked, almost unbelieving.

"Don't ask me. It was one of my greater achievements."

"Sam, thanks a million," Joe said. "Without you we would have been sunk."

"Forget it. When are you going to hit the Indian trail?"

"As soon as we rent a car," Frank said.

"Okay. I'll take the convertible to a shop and have it repaired," Sam went on. "All you have to do is pick it up later."

"Great!" Joe said. "Then are you going back home?"

"No. I'll stay here for a few days and check out the Magnitude Merchandising Mart. I want to meet that doll Chet's been talking about!"

Frank chuckled. "You might be marching into a lion's den. Better watch your step."

"Never fear. If you run into any trouble, call me at the Ohio."

"Will do. And thanks again, Sam!"

An hour later the boys set off in a rented hard-top. With Chet at the wheel, the Hardys relaxed and Joe studied the road map.

"We'll go through Hawk Head on our way to Yellow Springs," Joe said. "So let's stop at the Rideaus' for dinner."

Late in the afternoon they arrived in the little town. A gas-station attendant directed them to the Rideau home, which was Victorian gingerbread style, large and comfortable-looking. It was surrounded by wide sloping lawns. At the rear an old barn sat on a high knob of ground.

They pulled into the drive, got out, and stretched. Instantly a screen door banged open and the two German shepherds streaked out, barking.

"Hello, doggies," Chet said nervously. "Nice doggies . . ."

They raced toward him with muffled growls.

"Hey, look, we're friends," Frank said.

One of the dogs jumped up on Chet, and draped his forefeet over the boy's shoulders. Chet backed up, stumbled, and landed flat on his back. Frank made a dive for the car and Joe leaped for the lower limb of a nearby maple tree. He swung onto the branch and looked down on the other dog, who stood with his paws against the trunk.

As Chet struggled, Mrs. Rideau came out of the front door. "Tay! Boots! Come back here this instant!"

The animals turned and trotted toward their mistress. Chet got up groggily, Frank emerged from the car, and Joe jumped down from the tree.

"Hello, Mrs. Rideau," Frank said. "Do you remember us?"

"Why, of course," the woman replied. "Come on in. Don't mind these brutes. We need them to protect our home."

Joe wondered why, in a peaceful little town like Hawk Head, they needed that much protection. Chet brushed off his clothes and followed Frank and Joe into the old-fashioned living room.

"Please sit down," Mrs. Rideau said. "I'll get

the doctor. He's in the basement with his coins."

She left the room and the boys heard her footsteps going down the basement stairs.

Frank looked around. The room contained overstuffed, well-worn furniture. The walls were decorated with pictures, and certificates testifying that Dr. Rideau had won several prizes for his coin collection.

Footsteps sounded in the hall and the elderly man preceded his wife into the room. He was dressed in baggy slacks and a sport shirt with the sleeves rolled up to the elbows.

He shook hands with his callers. "Welcome to our home," he said and eased himself into one of the big armchairs. "We didn't expect to see you so soon."

"We're on our way to Yellow Springs," Frank said.

"Some business with the Indians?" the doctor asked, with a frown of disapproval.

"Yes," Joe said. "We have to do a little investigating for our father. He's a detective."

"Do you know anything about the Senecas at Yellow Springs?" Frank asked.

Their host shot a quick glance at his wife, clearing his throat. "Yes, we know about them. By the way, we got our car repaired, and it turned out it was tampered with!"

Frank realized the man was deliberately changing the subject. But before he could ask any questions, the doctor began to speak about his coin collection, which apparently was a tremendously valuable one.

"If you have any money to invest," he said with conviction, "put it into coins. They will never lose their value. Better than stocks and bonds—a hedge against inflation."

"You must have quite a treasure," Chet spoke up.

"Indeed I do! I have a vault in my cellar full of coins."

Joe gave a whistle. "Isn't it risky to have so much money around, Doctor?"

The doctor assured them that he was well-protected. The vault was made of concrete and steel and the combination was known only to him and his wife.

"And we have the dogs to protect us, too," Mrs. Rideau put in. "They are very friendly with people they know, but with strangers—"

"You don't have to tell us!" Chet blurted out. "One of them almost ate me up!"

Mrs. Rideau smiled. "Not really."

At that moment the animals pawed at the front door and Mrs. Rideau let them in. They lay down on the living-room rug, their front paws supporting their heads, and carefully watched the callers.

The doctor cleared his throat again. "To tell the truth, we had a little trouble recently."

"Trouble?" Frank asked. "Tell us about it."

The man said that ever since their return, they had noticed indications of someone trying to get into the house: sounds of prowlers and rattling door handles had awakened them at night. They had also found that a window screen had been jimmied.

"Thank goodness for the dogs," Mrs. Rideau said. "They scared away whoever it was."

"There seems to be a connection between the tampered car and these disturbances," Frank said. "Do you have any suspicions?"

"Yes!" Mrs. Rideau said emphatically. "The Senecas!"

"Why do you suspect the Indians?" Chet inquired.

"Because there is a rumor among them that I have their melted coins!" Dr. Rideau replied.

"Melted coins?" Joe repeated. "What good would they be to you? And what good are they to them?"

"They have no value for a collector whatever," answered the doctor. "And their gold value is not high. But I suppose the Indians feel that they are valuable."

"It was the Senecas all right," Mrs. Rideau said stubbornly. "We can't prove it, of course."

The boys did not know what to make of the strange story, but before Frank could ask any further questions, Mrs. Rideau said:

"I think you boys have heard enough about coins. Will you stay to dinner with us?"

"And it would hardly be advisable to continue your trip tonight," the doctor added. "You're welcome to stay till tomorrow."

"We'd love to have dinner with you," Frank said. "But don't bother making extra beds. We can put up at a motel."

"Nonsense," Dr. Rideau replied and launched into a lecture on thrift. "You'll never get rich spending money needlessly. Stay with us."

Chet immediately visualized a comfortable guest room with a soft feather bed upstairs. But that was not the plan. "You can sleep in the barn," the doctor went on. "We have tenants who occupy the second floor."

Mrs. Rideau headed for the kitchen. "Dinner will be on the table in a few minutes."

When they had eaten heartily of lamb chops, mashed potatoes, and broccoli, Joe felt he could sleep anywhere. He drove the car around to the barn, which had a sloping ramp leading up to the doors. The boys pulled them open and found folding cots with thin mattresses prepared for the night.

"The Waldorf it's not." Joe chuckled. "But I suppose it'll be all right."

"I'm so full and tired that I couldn't care less where I sleep," Chet said.

"Okay, let's go back and say good night to the Rideaus, then we'll turn in," Frank suggested.

As they walked toward the house the front door opened and two men walked out. They turned left and the boys did not get a good look at them.

When they asked Mrs. Rideau about them, she explained that the two men were Professors Mockton and Glade. "They have been staying with us for several months," she said.

"Professors?" Chet pricked up his ears.

"Yes. They are actually researchers," the woman replied. "They're studying the Indians— college professors, you know."

Before going back to the barn, Frank and Joe got flashlights from their car and laid them beside their cots. Then they settled down for the night. Chet could not get comfortable, finding his hips a little too broad for the narrow cot.

"We should have gone to a motel after all," he grumbled. Sitting up, he looked around in the gloom. He spied a pile of hay near the door. "That's better," he said. He threw his mattress on top of it and sank down into the hay.

Soon all was quiet, except for the even breathing of the boys. In the middle of the night Chet woke up. Something heavy was resting on his chest. His fingers explored cautiously and encountered coarse hair!

He yelled.

Frank and Joe sat bolt upright. "What's the matter, Chet?" Frank asked.

"Something's on my chest!"

The Hardys grabbed their lights and turned them on. The object on Chet was a grotesque red Indian mask. It was the ugliest face they had ever seen!

CHAPTER V

The Ghost Driver

CHET had been frightened by the feel of the hairy mask lying on his chest. Now, with the yellow glow of the flashlights full upon it, he picked it up with a sound of disgust.

The mask had horrible features—leering eyes made of copper, a large twisted nose, and a grotesque misshappen mouth. The hair was a long, white tangled mass.

"Holy Toledo!" Chet said. "Not the kind of think I like to wake up with!" He tossed it aside and leaped up.

Frank and Joe had already gotten out of bed and headed for the door. "Come on," said Joe. "Whoever left that pretty souvenir might still be around!"

With flashlights beaming, Frank circled the barn in one direction, Chet and Joe in the other. There was no one in sight. They carefully looked about a large forsythia bush and searched in the tall grass, but to no avail.

As they met in front of the barn Chet happened to glance toward the house. "Look, fellows!" he said, pointing to the second floor. They saw a faint glow of light flick off in one of the windows.

"Do you suppose it was those professors?" Chet asked.

Frank shrugged. "Why would they do a thing like that?"

The boys returned to the barn. Chet looked around for the mask. "Hey, which one of you guys took it?"

"Somebody must have come in here and taken it," Frank declared, "while we were searching outside!"

"Or else somebody has been hiding in here all along," Joe said.

Beaming their flashlights back and forth, they covered every cranny but found no one. Finally Chet settled back on his straw bed and tried to sleep.

"I think I'll hitchhike to Bayport," he said. "This place is too spooky for me."

"That's just what somebody wants us to do," Frank said. "If we get scared, we'll play directly into his hands."

"But why would anyone want to scare us?" Chet asked.

"Did it occur to you that this mask wasn't meant for us personally, but for any visitor the Rideaus might have?" Joe conjectured. "Whoever wants to get *them* out of the house might have done it."

"Who knows?" Frank said. "In any case I think one of us should stand guard for the rest of the night."

"I'll take the first watch," Joe volunteered, and soon the other two were asleep again. Two hours later Joe woke Frank, who took over.

About eight o'clock they all got up. They dressed and sat around till they saw Mrs. Rideau passing the kitchen window.

"Okay," Joe said. "Guess we can go in now."

"I've been thinking," Chet remarked on the way to the house, "It could have been the Senecas who played that little trick."

"Provided that the Rideaus' suspicions are correct," Joe said. "But we shouldn't jump to any conclusions."

"Let's not tell the Rideaus of this incident until we find out more about the Senecas," Frank put in.

The doctor and his wife greeted the boys with hearty good morning's and told them breakfast would be ready soon.

After washing up and brushing their hair, they sat around the table, enjoying ham and eggs.

Frank adroitly steered the conversation to the tenants upstairs. "I suppose they've left for their research work already," he said.

"Oh, yes. They left unusually early."

Frank and Joe exchanged glances, finished their breakfast, and pushed back their chairs. They thanked the Rideaus for their hospitality, then decided to go for a walk.

"It would be good to stretch our legs," Joe admitted. "Where are the dogs?"

"In the basement," Mrs. Rideau replied. "We thought it would be better while you're here."

The boys grinned and went outside.

"Come on," Frank said in a low voice. "Let's give that barn the once-over in daylight."

Joe climbed to the dusty hayloft with a pitchfork in his hand and pushed it gently through every pile of hay. It was evident nobody was hiding there.

Frank and Chet examined the stalls, apparently empty of horses for many years. They smelled of rotting hay, and decaying harnesses hung from pegs on the wall. No clues were uncovered.

"I still think those professors bear some investigating," Joe declared.

"You're right, but we have nothing to go on. Wish we could talk to them about their research. But we'd better be going."

The boys said good-by to the Rideaus and Joe headed the car toward the Senecas' ancestral lands. Through farmland, the road rose gradually to a high plateau.

Chet spotted a sign on a dirt road. *Zoar College!* An arrow pointed to the right toward the woods beyond the fields.

"Wait a minute!" Chet cried out. "What did I tell you? There is a Zoar College after all! Let's go see it."

"Okay," said Joe. He pulled into the dirt road. It dipped down, skirted a short knoll, and ended in a cul-de-sac.

"I don't see any college," Frank said.

The boys glanced around. Joe said, "It can't be that—that—" He pointed to two low buildings, which looked like overgrown chicken coops. The weeds grew almost to the windowsills, and the front door in one of the structures hung on a broken hinge.

The three got out of the car and walked over. A weather-beaten sign on the door proclaimed that it was, indeed, Zoar College.

"Aren't you glad you're not enrolled after all?" Frank asked Chet with a chuckle.

His friend was at a loss for words. He just shook his head in disbelief.

"Let's have a look around inside," Joe suggested.

The interior consisted of one large room. A blackboard was on one wall. On it a few mathematical problems were barely visible in moldering chalk. A desk laden with dust in the front of the room faced a dozen rickety chairs.

Chet sneezed sharply and a bird fluttered down from the rafters, streaking out the front door.

"That's the ornithology prof," Frank joked.

"What a racket!" Chet murmured.

"You know, this setup might be within the law," Frank said. "It provides some facilities and it is in the beautiful Zoar Valley, not far from Niagara Falls, just as the catalog pointed out."

"I wonder how many other guys were taken in by it," Chet muttered.

"Don't worry, we'll try to expose this outfit," Frank said and he looked about for evidence.

Joe poked among the scraps of paper on the floor. He found a sheet with sketches of Indian masks and Chet came up with a booklet stating that Indian lore was one of the courses given.

The boys studied the sketches. On the back of the sheet, in faint ink, was the name Nuremberg Museum. Next to it was the figure $5,000.

"I wonder what all this means," Frank said thoughtfully.

Chet shrugged and started to walk out the door. "Come on, fellows. I've seen enough," he said.

Just then they were startled by the sound of a motor. They dashed out to see their rented hard-top turning around and going down the road.

Chet gasped. "There's nobody at the wheel!" he exclaimed.

"That's the ornithology prof," Frank joked

The trio stopped short in surprise. The apparently driverless car churned up dust and disappeared around the knoll.

"Well," said Frank grimly, "I guess we'll walk!"

"I could kick myself for leaving the key in the ignition," Joe muttered. "But whoever thought there would be thieves out this way!"

"What thieves?" Chet demanded. "It was a ghost!"

"A ghost who ducked," Frank declared. "Come on. Let's get to the highway."

The Hardys strode up the hill with Chet puffing along behind. Emerging from the woods, they looked across the fields and could hardly believe what they saw! The car was parked near the highway! All three started to run.

"Let's not make any noise," Frank warned. "That 'ghost' might still be inside!"

Frank and Joe sneaked up on either side of the car. No one was in it, but on the seat lay a miniature Indian mask. It had a twisted nose and a wry mouth! Next to it was a scribbled note:

Hardys are evil spirits. We will drive you out!

CHAPTER VI

Masked Stowaway

Frank fingered the miniature false face. "Now it looks as if the Indians want to give us the old heave-ho," he said.

"I'm getting an inferiority complex," Joe complained. "Nobody wants us around!"

"So let's go home," Chet urged.

"What?" Joe asked in mock horror. "And miss Mother Jimerson's corn soup?"

"You've got a point there," Chet agreed. "Besides, you two were called the evil spirits, not me!"

The boys got into the car, and as Joe drove off, they mulled over the events of the last few minutes. Whoever had gone off with the automobile must have been a small fellow who had crouched low behind the wheel. But how did he get away?

"Maybe another car picked him up," Joe ventured.

"Or perhaps he's still lurking around here," suggested Chet.

"What I can't figure out," Frank said, "is why did the guy bother to move the car? He could have put the mask in without going through all that trouble."

"I suppose he wanted to give us a scare by apparently leaving us without transportation," Joe deduced.

"Well, from now on we'd better be very careful," said Frank.

Soon they passed a sign marked *Yellow Springs* and stopped at a small grocery to ask directions to Mrs. Jimerson's house. It turned out to be a small, one-story dwelling set far back from the road. A sign beside the driveway advertised the fact that the owner, Mrs. Jimerson, sold handwoven Indian baskets.

The boys drove up the lane and parked. As they approached the door, a stout woman with a round, ruddy face came out. Her hair, black but slightly graying, was pulled back into a braided bun. Her eyes crinkled when she smiled. "Would you like to buy some baskets?" she asked.

"Well, er—no," Frank said. "Are you Mrs. Jimerson?"

"Yes."

Frank mentioned her son in Cleveland and she beckoned them into a combination living room and workroom. Indian baskets were stacked up on one side. Most were completed, but others were in various stages of weaving. The boys glanced about, feeling a little uncomfortable at first because the woman did not speak. She just watched them. Finally she said, "Is my son Rod all right?"

"He's fine," Frank replied.

"A great guy with the steel girders," Chet put in. He sniffed a culinary aroma in the air and glanced at Joe. He was just about to say something about it, but Joe silently shook his head.

"Rod told us about Lendo Wallace," Frank spoke up, "and the disappearance of the Indian masks, Mrs. Jimerson. We're detectives."

"Oh?"

There was an awkward silence, but Mrs. Jimerson did not volunteer any information. Finally Chet said, "Something smells real good around here." His eyes rolled. "I think it might be corn soup!"

Mrs. Jimerson smiled. "Do you like corn soup?"

"You bet! It's my favorite!"

"Well"—Mrs. Jimerson studied Chet's plump, earnest face—"you shall have some."

She pulled three chairs to a table in one corner of the room and motioned for the boys to be seated. Then she went into the kitchen, and soon returned with a tray on which were three deep bowls of piping hot soup.

The young sleuths ate with relish, dipping in thick slices of homemade bread. Chet, who was finished first, looked appreciatively at Mrs. Jimerson.

"Would you like some more?" she asked.

At Chet's happy nod she quickly refilled the bowl. Then she began shyly to ask them questions. What were their names and where were they from? What were they doing in Seneca country and how did they happen to know about Rod?

Frank, as spokesman, gave her a general idea of their mission. "We'd like to help solve the mystery of the missing masks," he said.

The look on Mrs. Jimerson's face indicated that she might be opposed to outside interference.

Just then Joe glanced at Chet who was spooning the final mouthful of soup. "Chet, you look just like Spoon Mouth!" he quipped.

"No," Mrs. Jimerson objected. "Chet is a fine-looking boy and plump like boys should be!"

Frank and Joe laughed and so did Chet and the Indian woman. Now that she had relaxed, she began to talk more freely.

"Many years ago," she said, "near Lake Erie, lived a man who mistreated Indians. He had two joys in life, the quest for money and the harassment of the redskins in the area.

"One night his house burned down and he was consumed in the flames. Many people, knowing that he was rich, searched in vain for a cache of gold coins supposedly hidden in his house."

Wide-eyed, Chet blurted, "Were they found?"

"Not at first. But Indians finally found them."

"Great!" Joe said.

"Yes and no," Mrs. Jimerson continued. "The coins were melted, but strangely they were fused in the form of Spoon Mouth."

Frank and Joe exchanged excited glances. "You mean the melted coins and Spoon Mouth are one and the same?" Frank asked.

"Yes. I assumed you knew."

"What an odd coincidence," Chet said.

"Maybe not," Mrs. Jimerson continued. "The Indians felt that this had been done by their creator as a sign. The gold Spoon Mouth was carried into battle as their mascot and brought them exceptional luck. He was handed down from generation to generation."

"Hey, look!" Chet interrupted. He had been staring out of the window, idly watching their car. The trunk lid was opening slowly!

The boys crowded to the window. As the lid opened wider and wider, a slender figure emerged from the trunk and ran off. A nylon stocking had been pulled over his face to hide his features.

Frank, Joe, and Chet nearly fell over themselves, dashing for the door. Mrs. Jimerson looked on in surprise.

"Where'd he go?" Frank cried out.

"I think he ran over this way," Joe said, and dashed toward a neighboring yard.

Chet did not know which direction to take. He

stood still and looked all about. The intruder was built very much like Creepy, he thought, but why would he follow them to Yellow Springs?

Frank and Joe came back, panting. "He got away," Frank declared, "that's for sure. He must know this territory pretty well."

"Which would suggest that he was an Indian," said Joe.

"He looked like Creepy to me," Chet muttered.

They went back to their car and looked inside the trunk. Everything seemed to be in its place, the spare tire, the tool kit wrapped and secure next to the jack.

"So he didn't get a ride at the highway near Zoar College after all and came with us all the way to Yellow Springs," Frank said.

"What a nut!" Joe shook his head.

The boys apologized to Mrs. Jimerson for running off and explained what had happened. They seated themselves at the table again, waiting for her to relate more of the legend about Spoon Mouth.

She said that the golden relic had been kept at the new Seneca longhouse, a modern frame building nearby.

"Then he was stolen," she said sadly. "We don't know who did it. But many of our people feel now that the tribe is in disfavor with the spirits."

"Mrs. Jimerson," Frank said, "do you have any suspicion at all as to who took the relic?" The woman did not answer right away. Finally she shrugged and said, "No. No suspicions."

"Can you tell us some more about Lendo Wallace, the head of the False Face Society?" Frank went on. "Rod mentioned him briefly and—"

Just then a fierce explosion ripped the air and rattled the windows!

CHAPTER VII

No Admittance, Please!

THE boys and Mrs. Jimerson were momentarily stunned by the blast. They looked out the window and saw that the trunk lid of the Hardys' car had blown open.

"Come on!" Frank cried out.

The three boys hastened outside.

"Oh, no!" Joe exclaimed. "What a mess!"

The back seat was blown out, their luggage ripped open, the trunk cover a total loss and a tire punctured.

The Indian woman came out of the house, shaking her head. "What in the world happened?" she asked.

"Somebody's plenty mad at us," Frank said grimly.

"You've been asking too many embarrassing questions," Chet said. "Especially in Cleveland.

Could be the Zoar College people are worried that you'll expose their racket."

"No doubt we were supposed to be in the car when the charge went off," Frank mused.

"And in the hospital now," Joe added.

Frank turned to Mrs. Jimerson. "Do you think the Senecas have something against us?"

"No, of course not. Why should they?"

Frank inspected the car again. "The bomb was probably hidden in the tool kit," he said. "Well, let's see if she's still running."

He turned the key and found out that the mechanical workings, fortunately, were not damaged.

The boys thanked Mrs. Jimerson for her hospitality. Chet assured her that the corn soup was the best he had ever tasted. Then they climbed into the front seat and drove off.

"We'll have to find a motel," Frank said. "And then I suggest that one of us drive this car back to Cleveland and pick up our own."

"I'll go," Chet volunteered.

"Okay," said Frank. He drove to a long, low building bearing the name Sunset Motel. It advertised fourteen rooms and two suites.

As they applied at the desk for accommodations, the affable manager smiled. "You're kind of early, aren't you?" he said.

Frank looked blank. "What do you mean?"

"Aren't you college boys? Several students from

Zoar College stayed here last summer," the man replied. He jerked his thumb toward the back of the motel. "One of them left his motorcycle behind."

Joe snapped his fingers. "That may answer a question for us," he said. "We're going to need transportation. Our friend is taking the car back to Cleveland where we rented it."

"Is the motorcycle in working order?" Frank asked.

"I think so. It was kept under a tarpaulin all winter."

"May we use it?"

"Help yourselves, fellows."

The boys took their broken baggage to their room, then said good-by to Chet, who set off for Ohio.

"The car is undoubtedly covered by insurance," Frank told him. "If there is any trouble about it, have the rental company contact Sam Radley."

Chet waved as he drove away and Joe turned to his brother. "What now, fearless leader?"

"I'd say Lendo Wallace is next on our list. We'll beard the lion in his den."

"Okay, let's see if we can get this motorcycle started."

They walked around to the back of the motel, pulled the tarpaulin off the machine, then checked the spark plugs and the gas tank.

"No reason why she shouldn't turn over," Joe declared as he wheeled the cycle toward the driveway in front of the motel.

He got on and kicked it a couple of times. The machine backfired, sending out a puff of white smoke. On the next try Joe was successful. At first the noisy engine sounded like a helicopter, then settled down to a throaty roar.

Frank, meanwhile, had gone inside to get directions for Lendo Wallace's place. He returned, hopped on the back, and they shot off down the road. Soon they reached the lane leading to Wallace's house. It was more of a shack than Mrs. Jimerson's and the Hardys felt sorry for the way some Indians had to live.

The two dismounted, set the machine on the kickstand, and approached the shanty.

"This job may be ticklish," Joe said.

Frank nodded as they strode on. "All the same, let's not beat around the bush."

They knocked on the screen door. A man pushed it open and stepped outside. He was short with a tanned face and square shoulders. His general appearance was one of lean agility.

"Mr. Wallace?" Frank asked.

The man nodded.

Frank introduced himself and Joe, then said, "We'd like to talk with you. May we come in?"

Lendo Wallace eyed them coolly. "If you have something to discuss, we can do it out here."

The hostility in his voice indicated that getting information from the Indian was going to be more difficult than they had anticipated.

"All right," Frank said. "We'll talk out here."

Seeing a chopping block with a hatchet bedded in its surface, he walked over to it and sat down casually.

Wallace glared at him for a moment, but when Joe hunkered down beside his brother, the Indian relaxed a bit and said, "All right. Talk. What do you want?"

Frank decided to aim the first question right on target. "Mr. Wallace," he said, "what do you know about Spoon Mouth?"

The Indian stiffened. His eyes darted from one boy to the other. The only reply was a shrug. Before the Hardys had a chance to ask another question, a chauffeured Cadillac drove slowly past Wallace's shack. It stopped two hundred yards down the road, turned about, and came back again.

A youth in the back seat was leaning out the window. He cupped his hands and shouted something unintelligible.

"What does he want?" asked Joe.

The youth tapped the chauffeur on the shoulder, said something, and the limousine drove on.

"What was that all about?" said Frank, scratching his head.

"Maybe that guy thought he knew us," Joe suggested.

The young detectives turned their attention to Wallace once more. He was scowling. "I don't intend to talk about Spoon Mouth or anything else," he declared.

"It's very important to your tribe that the golden relic be found, isn't it?" Joe asked.

"It is," the Indian had to admit. His eyes were deeply troubled.

"Do you know how it was stolen?" Frank asked.

"No."

"What about the disappearance of the false faces?" said Joe. "Can't you give us some idea what's going on around here?"

Wallace's face grew taut, and he said, "If the police cannot find out, how do you expect to?" Before the boys could reply, he added, "It is none of your business anyhow, nor Rod Jimerson's either!"

The Hardys were dumbfounded.

"How did you know Rod sent us?" Frank demanded.

Wallace shrugged. "I guessed it. He's been bugging me about this all along." With that he turned on his heels and went inside his shack.

"Well, he wasn't very informative," Joe said.

"He's so hostile you'd think he stole the masks himself," Frank declared.

"I don't know," Joe replied. "He looks as if he's in bad trouble. But somehow he doesn't strike me as a thief."

Frank got on the motorcycle, grabbed the handle bars, and Joe vaulted on the seat behind him. With a powerful growl, the machine leaped ahead and they enjoyed the cool breeze whipping their faces as they rode toward the motel.

When they reached it they noticed a Cadillac standing in front of one of the suites.

"Hey, Frank! It looks like the one that passed us before!" Joe shouted over the roar.

Frank nodded. Smoothly he applied the brakes and the cycle rolled toward a stop. Before either of the boys could dismount, a young man stepped into view. He was older than the Hardys, perhaps nineteen or twenty, thickset, with black hair and an unsmiling face.

He took a few quick steps forward, lunged at Joe, and struck him on the shoulder. The Hardys lost their balance and were spilled to the ground. The motorcycle fell on top, pinning them to the driveway!

CHAPTER VIII

A Flattened Foe

WINCING with pain, Frank and Joe untangled themselves from the fallen bike. They limped to their feet, righted the cycle, and brushed the dust from their clothes.

Joe had suffered the most damage. His right leg and arm were skinned. His chafed elbow smarted and blood oozed through his shirt.

Angrily the boys walked toward the perpetrator of the mean trick, who stood and smirked.

"Now what was the big idea?" Frank asked sharply.

Joe was hot with indignation. He clenched his fists and pressed past him. "Why ask any questions, Frank? Let me sock the jerk!"

Frank put out an arm and held Joe back. "Easy now. I'll handle this." He turned.

"Why did you knock us down?" he demanded, standing nose to nose with the larger boy, who wore an expression of childish amusement.

"You were riding my cycle without permission," he said finally.

"*Your* cycle?" Joe said. "Why, we—"

The motel manager, having heard the commotion, hastened up to the trio. "I can explain everything," he said. "I gave them permission to use the bike!"

The youth looked at him coldly. "You knew it belonged to me, didn't you?"

"It's been around here a long time. I thought you wouldn't mind."

"You were wrong!" the youth said haughtily.

The manager backed off and returned to his office.

"Come on, Joe," Frank said. "Let's go."

They strode to their room and closed the door.

"I don't see how you could take that," Joe said.

"Listen, Joe. We're here to do a job," Frank declared. "Getting into a big hassle won't help us at all."

Joe pulled off his clothes and stepped into the shower. The hot water stung his abrasions, but the bleeding had stopped. He was toweling himself gingerly when the phone rang.

Frank picked it up. It was the manager, who was full of apologies. The youth, he said, was Elmont Chidsee. He had been going to Zoar College for three summers and was to be graduated this year.

"He had an awful nerve knocking us off the

bike like that," Frank said. "Maybe Joe should have bopped him after all."

The man explained that Chidsee was an indolent type who spent most of his time loafing on a fat allowance from a rich uncle.

"He thinks he's great, all right," Frank said, and added, "Why in the world would anybody come for three years to a phony place like Zoar?"

"Because no other school would have him," the manager replied. "Well, I hope your brother is okay." With that he hung up.

Frank relayed the information to Joe, then he stripped and stepped into the shower. When both boys were dressed again, a bold knock sounded on the door. Joe opened it to see Chidsee standing there, the same smirk on his face.

Joe was surprised by the visit, and his face showed it.

"Don't worry," Chidsee said. "I'm not going to hurt you."

"How nice of you!" Joe replied sarcastically. "What do you want?"

"You broke my bike!"

"No kidding!"

"I want you to fix it!"

"Fix it yourself!"

"He probably doesn't know how," Frank put in. "We'll do it!"

His matter-of-fact tone puzzled the Zoar student.

"Most likely some dust in the ignition," Frank went on, and the Hardys walked over to the motorcycle. Frank checked it out, and in no time at all had it running again.

Chidsee looked on all the while, with an envious half-smile. He curled his lips. "You fellows seem to know just what to do. Maybe you loused it up on purpose."

"Of course, of course," Frank said, wiping his hands on a piece of cloth. "We do this all the time!"

There was no word of thanks from Chidsee. Instead, he declared imperiously, "Now remember, keep your hands off what doesn't belong to you!"

Joe's lips tightened. "Same goes for you, Chidsee!" he said, putting a hand on his left shoulder. "This, for instance, belongs to me. So stay away!"

Elmont Chidsee sneered and moved in on Joe. "Oh, yeah? How would you like the other one pushed?"

Frank quickly stepped between them.

"Out of my way!" Chidsee growled.

Frank realized that argument was futile. With lightning speed he whipped a left hand into Elmont's midsection.

"*Oof!*" Chidsee doubled over, only to meet a stiff right-hand uppercut to his chin.

With glazed eyes he staggered backward on rubbery legs. He stumbled over his own feet and sat down on the pavement.

Just then another car drove into the motel parking area. It stopped and a man leaned out the window to observe the ludicrous look on Chidsee's face. He chuckled, turned his head to Frank, and said, "Wow! What a belt!"

Chidsee's chauffeur came out of their suite to see what had happened. He ran over to the boy and helped him to his feet. Elmont Chidsee rubbed his chin, grimaced at the pain, and muttered to the Hardys, "I'll get even with you for this!"

"We're looking forward to seeing you again, chum!" Joe said with a grin.

The chauffeur took Chidsee's arm and pulled him into their apartment. The door slammed shut.

"Nice going, Frank!" Joe praised his brother.

"He had it coming," Frank replied. "Maybe he'll lay off now."

"I doubt it."

For the rest of the day the Hardys studied a map of the area, familiarizing themselves completely with Yellow Springs and the Indian Reservation.

Their sympathetic motel host was a great help. He pointed out whatever the boys wanted to know.

"One thing we need," Joe said that evening, "is some kind of transportation."

"With luck," Frank said, "Chet ought to be

back tomorrow. Or at least the day after. Meanwhile, we'll spy on Wallace."

The next morning, the boys put on dark trousers and each selected a green sport shirt, to look as inconspicuous as possible in their sleuthing.

The small motel dining room provided a hearty breakfast. Frank and Joe looked around for Chidsee and his chauffeur, but they had not yet appeared.

"They probably get room service," Frank said with a chuckle.

"Who knows? With his sore jaw Chidsee might not be able to eat at all," Joe replied.

"It wouldn't hurt him to lose some of his blubber around the middle," Frank said. "He's not in such good condition."

The boys got a stack of sandwiches and a canteen of water from the kitchen, then hiked along the road to Wallace's place. On the way they discussed Chidsee.

"How can a guy spend all his time driving around with a chauffeur!" Joe said. "I wonder if he has any friends."

"I heard jokes about boys with rich uncles," Frank said humorously, "but I've never met one before."

"He certainly is a spoiled brat," Joe remarked.

Traffic was light, but the Hardys kept an eye peeled for Wallace, also for the masked attacker who had blown up their car, and for Chidsee.

"I expect more trouble from him," Joe said. "If his Caddy comes along, dive for cover!"

"Look, there's Wallace's house," Frank said a few seconds later and pointed.

The two moved off the road and into a shallow ditch, screened on all sides by grass and tall weeds.

Frank reasoned that Wallace, having been alerted by their investigation, would probably contact a confederate, if, indeed, he was mixed up in the disappearance of the masks.

"Watch it!" Joe cautioned.

As they peered through the weeds the door of the shack opened. The Indian stepped out, holding a small hatchet in his right hand. A knife was tucked inside his belt. He looked about, then moved toward the woods at the back of his property.

"Come on. Let's follow him," Frank said.

Wallace glanced back several times, but the Hardys were on the alert and dropped to the grass unseen. Once among the tall trees, cover was better.

Frank and Joe kept Wallace's bobbing figure in sight. They crouched low and were careful not to step on crackling twigs. Finally the Indian stopped and surveyed a basswood tree.

Joe whispered, "He's not going to cut it down with that little hatchet, is he?"

"No. Look!"

The man raised his hatchet and with deft

strokes began to chip into the smooth bark. Then he put the hatchet down, pulled out his knife, and with elbows held tightly against the trunk for leverage, he used both hands to carve into the wood.

The Hardys advanced as close as they could, fascinated by the skill of the carver. With long, curving strokes he fashioned a crooked nose, then the wry, lopsided mouth.

Joe pressed close to Frank's ear. "That's the same kind of mask that scared Chet in the barn!" he whispered.

Wallace stopped abruptly. He wheeled around, looked hard, and listened. The boys held their breath and remained absolutely motionless. Then Wallace returned to work.

Frank beckoned to Joe, and they backed off into the woods.

"What fantastic hearing that fellow has," said Joe when they were safely away from the area.

"You nearly blew our cover!"

"Sorry about that," Joe replied, and added, "Maybe he specializes in that Broken Nose mask. Do you suppose he's the one that put Old Horror Puss on top of Chet that night?"

"It's a possibility," Frank admitted.

They retreated to the edge of the woods and kept a vigil until Lendo Wallace came out and strode back to his house.

The stakeout became tedious as the day wore

on. The Indian had no visitors, nor did he go out again.

By sundown they had eaten all their sandwiches and had drunk the last drop of water. Under cover of darkness Frank and Joe stretched from their cramped positions.

"Boy, that feels good!" Joe said. "How long do you think we should keep our vigil?"

"Until he goes to bed," Frank decided. "Come on. Maybe we can have a look inside through one of the windows."

Just as they were sneaking up to the house for closer surveillance, a couple of headlights stabbed their beams along the lane and a car pulled up beside the shack.

The boys ducked, and a man got out and hastened inside.

"Oh, boy!" Joe whispered. "Looks as if we hit pay dirt!"

"Right. Maybe we can pick up a clue."

They waited for a while cautiously, then inched their way toward the house. Slowly they moved around the outside to an open window.

At that instant the shade was drawn. It flapped lightly in the evening breeze, but completely hid all within.

Frank and Joe lifted their heads to get a glimpse of the caller. No luck. The indistinguishable murmur of conversation came to their ears. Then the talk grew louder. Anger edged the words of the visitor.

"Now look here!" he said emphatically. "You deliver the full amount we agreed on or the deal is off!"

"But the tribe!" Wallace pleaded. "I have to think of my people. Don't you understand that?"

"I understand you made a deal. And a deal is a deal!" The speaker pounded his fist hard on the table.

The sudden jar caused the shade to fly up with a bang.

Frank and Joe were in full view!

CHAPTER IX

A Close Call

SURPRISE was instant and complete! Frank and Joe ducked and scrambled into the cover of some bushes. They had seen two persons, but in that split second could not identify Lendo Wallace's visitor.

"Oh, nuts," said Joe. "They saw us!"

"I don't think the stranger did," Frank said. "He had his back turned."

"Let's get a look at that license number," Joe suggested. "Quick!"

As the boys crept toward the car, the back door opened and the two men rushed out. Frank and Joe melted back into the shadows.

Wallace was quiet, but his visitor muttered angrily as they circled the house once, then again. The stranger zigzagged with his flashlight in a frantic effort to spot the eavesdroppers.

The Hardys crawled backward, and tried to pick up all the information they could. Finally the flashlight clicked off and a voice said, "They got away. Did you see who they were?"

"No," Wallace replied. "I didn't see."

"Were they some of your Senecas?"

"I didn't see," Wallace insisted.

The two men walked over to the car, where they talked for a while. Frank and Joe decided not to take further risks of discovery. Keeping to one side of the road, they moved out of sight, then trudged back to their motel.

It was well lighted, and they were still some distance away when they noticed Elmont Chidsee. He sat on a folding chair near their door.

"Now what do you make of that?" Joe asked.

"Obviously he's standing guard."

Joe grinned. "The spies are being spied on."

"Let's play a little trick on him," Frank suggested. Quickly he explained his plan to Joe.

The boys crept closer, circled around to one side of the motel, and hid behind the big air-conditioning unit. Chidsee rose from the chair, walked impatiently up and down for a few minutes, then seated himself again.

"I wonder how long he's been there," asked Joe.

"I assume quite a while," said Frank. "He's getting restless."

"Okay, let's go around back," Joe urged.

They moved cautiously to the rear. Frank pulled out his pocketknife and snapped open the

Frank noiselessly slid the window open

screwdriver blade. Carefully he pried one side of the window, then the other. It budged a quarter-inch. He noiselessly slid the window open and both crawled inside.

Quietly they undressed and put their pajamas on.

"Here's where we have some fun with our sentry," Frank whispered. He stood near the door, put his hand on the knob, and announced in a loud voice, "Hey, Joe, it's getting awful hot in here. I think I'll go out for a breath of air."

He opened the door quickly. Chidsee nearly fell off his chair in amazement. His jaw dropped.

"Well, well. If it isn't our long-lost friend," Frank said. "What are you doing here?"

No answer. Chidsee stared at him in bewilderment, muttered something, and hastened off.

Frank closed the door and the boys had a good laugh. "He didn't know he was being a babysitter," Joe chortled.

"You can't blame the poor guy for being surprised," Frank said. Then he became serious. "Joe, I smell a rat!"

"You were pretty close to him," Joe said, still in a jovial mood.

"He's in league with somebody else—most likely the people who've been harassing us all along. They put him here to stand watch—maybe they were expecting us to spy on Wallace tonight!"

"You could be right," Joe retorted. "If Chidsee could have reported the time we returned, that guy who was browbeating Wallace surely would have known that we were the eavesdroppers."

"But the game isn't over yet," Frank said, and started dressing. "Come on. We have some more work to do."

The two climbed out of the window again. Bending low, they crept around the rear of the motel till they were directly below the window of Chidsee's apartment.

"Listen!" Frank whispered.

From inside came muffled voices.

"They were in their room all the time!" Chidsee whined. "In their pajamas. Must have gone to bed early!"

The chauffeur mumbled something the boys could not understand. Then they heard the door open and slam shut.

"What are you doing in here, Elmont? Didn't I tell you to stand guard?" said a harsh voice.

"I did!"

"What do you mean, you did?"

"They've been inside all night!"

"Are you sure?" The visitor sounded incredulous.

"If you don't believe me, go look for yourself."

The chauffeur spoke up. "You guys better be quiet, or the whole motel will know what you're up to!"

The sounds of conversation sank immediately. Frank and Joe listened intently, their hearts pounding. Even though the voices inside were mumbled and unintelligible, the boys dared not speak.

Then the caller became annoyed and raised his voice once more. "Now look, give it back!"

"I don't have it here," Chidsee replied pettishly.

"Where is it?"

"Don't worry, you'll get it!"

"We need it now, uncle or no uncle. Don't forget, I have a deal cooking. You better shape up or else!"

Just then the phone rang. The stranger picked it up, and after a crisp "hello" talked low. The Hardys could barely make out what was being said.

"A couple of Senecas have been spying on us," he said. There was silence for a few seconds. "We've got to be careful and wind this up fast."

Silence once more. Then the door slammed and the visitor was gone.

Frank tugged his brother's arm and they hurried around to the front to get a look at the man. But he was already in his car and sped off into the night.

Frank and Joe returned to their room by way of the window and discussed the case.

"That sounded a lot like the guy who visited Lendo Wallace tonight," Joe remarked.

"It must have been," Frank agreed. "He said that the Senecas were spying on him."

"And he probably knows that Rod Jimerson and others are suspicious of Wallace because he's done nothing about the mask thefts."

"What's wrong with Wallace, anyway?" Joe asked, frowning. "We know he's made some kind of deal with the fellow who's also a buddy of Chidsee's—but what is it?"

Frank shrugged. "Who knows? Maybe he's stealing the missing masks himself! He might even have taken Spoon Mouth!"

"He must need money awful bad," Joe said, "to betray his own people."

"I don't know. Come on. Let's hit the sack," said Frank. "I'm weary."

In pajamas once again, the boys were soon fast asleep.

When they opened the draw curtains the next morning, the sun streamed into their room. They had slept until nine o'clock! Yawning and squinting, Joe glanced down the motel facade to Chidsee's suite. The Cadillac was gone.

"They've flown the coop already, Frank," he reported, and opened the door. The maid walked by. Joe beckoned to her. "Have Mr. Chidsee and his chauffeur left?" he asked.

The chubby woman, carrying a vacuum and a dustcloth, said Yes. She was going to make up the rooms for the day.

Joe said quickly, "My brother and I will be dressed in a minute, and we might have company later. Will you make ours first?"

"Sure. I'll be right back." The maid left. Frank and Joe quickly splashed cold water on their faces, put on their clothes, and walked out. Casually they sauntered to Chidsee's suite. The door stood ajar.

"Okay, Joe. Now's our chance," Frank said and slipped into the living room.

Joe followed close behind. Quickly they took in the scene. Crushed cigarette butts littered the floor, empty soda cans stood on the table, and in the adjoining room the beds were unmade and towels strewn about.

"Neat people," Joe commented sarcastically as they scouted the place for possible clues. Nothing turned up in the living room, and the bedroom proved equally void of any personal belongings.

Joe checked the blotter on the writing desk. No ink marks were on it. Frank, meanwhile, picked through the wastebasket. As he took out a folded newspaper, a crumpled piece of paper fell out from between the pages.

Then they heard footsteps outside. Frank quickly pulled Joe into the bedroom. The footsteps stopped in front of the apartment door.

"Maybe it's the maid," Joe said. "Wouldn't it be embarrassing if she found us here?"

"It sounded like a man's steps," Frank replied, "and it would be even more embarrassing if it's Chidsee himself."

"Let's try the bathroom window," Joe advised. They heard muffled voices, then someone walked away from the suite. The boys listened intently for a moment, then went back into the living room. Frank picked up the piece of paper, hastened to the desk, and spread it flat.

On the paper, written in pencil, were the words *Prof called,* and a phone number.

Frank whistled softly. "What a clue, Joe!"

Just then the boys heard a noise behind them. They wheeled around to see Lendo Wallace framed in the doorway. His hand went to the knife in his belt!

CHAPTER X

Surprise Connection

STARING at them in the doorway, Lendo Wallace seemed more startled than the Hardys. Had the Indian expected to see Elmont Chidsee?

"What are you doing here?" he finally asked.

"Looking around," Frank replied in a matter-of-fact tone.

Wallace's hand dropped from the knife haft and he stepped toward the Hardys with an inquisitive stare. "This isn't your room, is it?"

"No. It belongs to Elmont Chidsee and his chauffeur."

"I assume you were looking for him," Joe put in. "Chidsee and his buddy who was here last night, perhaps?"

His bold approach had the desired effect. Wallace's eyes widened and his lips moved but he said nothing. As he turned to go, Joe shot another question.

"Why the knife in your belt, Mr. Wallace?"

"I'm going to cut a tree; that is, cut a mask in a tree." The Indian's voice seemed less hostile.

"I understand that's an ancient art with the Six Nations," Frank said, trying to draw out the Seneca.

It seemed to be the right approach. Lendo Wallace relaxed a little and began to talk about the art of carving false faces. As he spoke, all three walked from Chidsee's apartment and stood outside.

"Each mask," Wallace said, "is designed to chase certain evil spirits."

"I've seen a very frightening one," Frank remarked. "It had a crooked nose and a sideways mouth."

"You mean Old Broken Nose. He's quite fierce, especially with the horsetail hair."

"So that was it," Frank thought. "The streaming white hair which scared Chet actually was a horsetail!" He probed deeper with his next statement.

"A friend of ours was frightened by a Broken Nose mask one night!"

Wallace looked blank. Frank concluded that he was not the one who had been at the Rideaus' barn during their first visit.

Wallace continued with his favorite subject. "Young Indians don't care about masks any more," he said sadly. "They aren't interested. You send them out to cut some wood and they don't know willow from bass."

Joe looked at the Indian's jalopy. It was the same year as Chet's. "We have a friend who has a car just like this," Joe said with a grin. "Does yours backfire much?"

For the first time Wallace smiled. "Enough to scare horses," he replied.

Now the chill was thawing more. Frank asked Wallace what he did for a living. The Indian told him that he made snow snakes—long sticks which boys hurled over the ice in a game; also lacrosse sticks, turtle-shell rattles, and headdresses.

"Our people play a lot of lacrosse," he said. "The game originated with Northern Indians. This work keeps me busy all winter, and I sell my wares in the summertime."

Suddenly animation left the man's face as if a switch had been turned off. He fixed both boys with his gaze and said icily, "Why were you spying on me last night?"

Frank and Joe were taken aback. So he had seen their faces at the window! Yet he had not given them away!

Caught flat-footed, they fumbled for a reply, but Wallace spared them the effort. He jumped into his car, started the motor, and sped out of the motel drive onto the main highway.

Frank shook his head. "Joe, that man is an enigma."

"You said it! I certainly can't figure him out, but I'm beginning to think he's a thief. Did you see how neatly he set us up for that question about spying?"

"He's no fool. He toyed with us. And he's got some connection with Chidsee!"

Chagrined, the Hardys returned to their own room. The maid had just finished and excused herself as she brushed past them on their way in.

Frank sank into a chair while Joe flopped down on the bed.

"Score for Lendo Wallace," Frank said ruefully. "You can't win 'em all!"

"What I want to know," Joe said, "is why he didn't tell his visitor who we were."

"Well, he's obviously playing some kind of double game!"

"Maybe he likes us," Joe said with a chuckle.

"Maybe he does. His hostility could be a front, you know."

"Oh, sure! The heart of gold underneath it all!" Joe said sarcastically, but his brother reminded him that the Indian seemed to be in some serious trouble.

"Even if we could help him, he'd never let us," Joe stated.

"I know," Frank replied. "But Wallace's problem might be the key to the whole Spoon Mouth affair."

"Well," Joe said, "at least we have one clue."

"Right. Let's follow it up right away," Frank said. He pulled the crumpled note from his pocket. Both studied the phone number on it.

"What's your guess?" Frank asked, walking to the telephone.

"I'd say Zoar College," Joe replied half-jestingly.

"How about Chidsee's rich uncle?" Frank shot back. "What'll I say if *he's* the guy at the other end of the wire?"

"That's your problem," Joe replied cheerfully. "Maybe you could ask him to pay damages since his lovable nephew threw us off the motorcycle!"

Frank dialed the number. *What would he say?*

"I'll have to play it by ear," he thought as the phone rang at the other end. Then someone lifted the receiver and a woman's voice said, "Hello?"

"Er—hello," Frank replied. "I have a message here to call this number. Is this 677–3408?"

"That's right," the woman replied. "Whom do you wish to speak to?"

"Well, thank you, I think I must have the wrong—"

"Aren't you one of the Hardy boys?" the woman interrupted.

"Yes—er—Frank Hardy. Who are you?"

"Mrs. Rideau, of course. I didn't realize you had our telephone number."

"Neither did I," Frank replied drily.

Luckily Mrs. Rideau did not seem surprised at the whole thing. She seemed rather excited, however. "Frank, I'm so glad you called."

"Why is that, Mrs. Rideau?"

"The doctor and I need your help as detectives."

"What's happened?"

"The Indians have tried to break into our house twice since you left. Please, can you come to Hawk Head as soon as possible?"

"Sure. But we have no car. Right now we're at the Sunset Motel, and it might take us a little while to get there!"

"There's a bus," Mrs. Rideau said. "It stops near the motel. What happened to your car?"

"That's a long story. Do the local police know about the Indians?" Frank asked.

"Yes, we notified them."

"Good. Joe and I will get over as soon as we can." Frank hung up and turned to Joe. He shook his head slowly. "How about that!"

"The prof referred to in the phone message is one of Mrs. Rideau's tenants!" Joe exclaimed. "And he's connected with Elmont Chidsee, who's connected with Zoar College!"

"It's likely, therefore, the prof teaches at Zoar," Frank completed the train of thought.

"I wonder if he's the one who came to see Wallace and later Chidsee last night," Joe said.

"We can't be sure about anything. Anyway, going back to the Rideaus will give us a chance to talk to their tenants, and perhaps we can identify the voice!"

The boys quickly packed their bags and wrote a note for Chet, saying that if he returned before they did, he should stay and wait for them.

Frank phoned the motel manager and told him they would be out of town for a while, but wanted to keep their room. He added, "And if Chet Morton comes back, don't let him get away!"

Then he inquired about the Hawk Head bus, and was informed that one would pass the Sunset Motel in exactly half an hour. When he had hung up, Frank snapped his fingers.

"Listen, Joe. Half an hour will give us time to go to Lendo Wallace's place."

"What for?"

"Well, we suspect he's in trouble. So I'm going to offer our help."

"You know he'll turn you down."

"We can give it a try, right?"

"Okay."

They left their room, putting their bags just inside the door for handy pickup when they returned from Wallace's house. Then they hiked along the road briskly, and turned down the lane to the Indian's shack.

"Mr. Wallace!" Frank called out. There was no reply. Obviously the Indian was not home.

The Hardys walked up to the front door. It was covered with a chalk drawing of Old Broken-Nose. Under it was a warning message:

Hardys: Danger ahead! Leave Yellow Springs at once!

CHAPTER XI

Footsteps in the Dark

"THAT's a strange kind of warning," Frank said. "It doesn't threaten us, just says get out because there's danger ahead."

"Sounds more like a friend than an enemy," Joe had to admit.

"That's Wallace for you," Frank went on, glancing about to see if anyone were observing them. "He's inscrutable. You don't know if he's for you or against you."

As Joe stood fascinated by the twisted countenance of the Indian mask, Frank put his hand on the doorknob and turned it. The hinges squeaked as the door opened an inch or so.

"He doesn't keep the place locked," Frank remarked.

"In that case, maybe he's hiding around here and watching us," Joe said.

"Could be," Frank replied. "But we have no time to look for him now." He glanced at his watch. "We'd better go or we'll miss the bus."

Frank closed the door, gave the leering face final glance, then trotted alongside his brother back to the motel. They grabbed their bags and walked to the road in time to see the bus coming in the distance.

When they got aboard the near-empty vehicle, they thrust their luggage on a seat, then sat back to watch the scenery.

"This is the life," said Joe. He laced his fingers behind his neck, leaned back, and closed his eyes. "No hot-rod hoods, no vandals, no creeps . . ."

He was jerked out of his reverie by a poke in the ribs. "Forget it," said Frank. "Look out the window!"

Joe opened his eyes in time to see a sleek Cadillac gliding past at a speed well above the limit. He groaned.

"There goes our boy Elmont," said Frank. "I wonder where to."

"He just can't bear to be away from us," Joe muttered. "Or maybe he's on his way to his uncle for another handout."

Frank had serious thoughts about Chidsee. His car, too, was headed in the direction of Hawk Head. Might trouble be brewing there? Was he on his way to the Rideau house to contact the professors?

Frank's thoughts drifted away as the humming tires and the passing scenery lolled him into a drowsy mood. He felt his head nod and dozed.

All of a sudden the bus brakes screeched and the Hardys were pitched forward, banging their heads on the seats in front of them.

Joe's first thought was the Cadillac. Had it deliberately tried to wreck the bus?

The few other passengers, two of them thrown in the aisle, protested with shouts of anger. The Hardys left their seats and walked to the front.

"What happened?" Frank asked the embarrassed driver, who shook his head in disgust. He pointed to the roadside, where a flock of geese were waddling up the slope.

"That's what!" he replied. "They don't care if anyone's coming! I'd have had a fine bill to pay if I had sent their feathers flying."

Frank and Joe took their seats again and Frank said, "See? Never a dull moment in Indian country."

"Oh, quit the corn, Frank," Joe said.

"Well, Chet would have liked it," Frank said in mock protest.

"Which reminds me," Joe went on, "he should be arriving at the motel any moment with our car. I hope he doesn't run into Wallace alone."

"Don't worry. He'll probably spend his time at Mrs. Jimerson's, eating her corn soup till he busts!"

Finally, as the bus passed over the brow of the hill, the brothers saw Hawk Head in the distance. They were let off in the center of town and walked briskly toward the Rideau house. When they approached the place, the two dogs leaped playfully on them and they had to fend off their powerful bodies like defensive linemen on a football team.

"Down, fellows!" Frank ordered.

The German shepherds obeyed, and barking, circled the boys as they walked toward the doorway. Joe glanced up at the second floor. A curtain on one of the windows parted slightly.

"Don't look now, Frank, but someone's playing peekaboo upstairs," he said.

"I wonder if they do that every time somebody comes to the house," Frank muttered.

The noise brought Mrs. Rideau to the door. "Oh, I'm so glad you came so soon," she said. "Doctor and I are having such trouble." She ushered the Hardys into the living room, where her husband sat at a table, examining a pile of coins with a magnifying glass.

"Hello, boys," he greeted them. "Have you been thinking over my idea of investing in coins as the safest possible business venture?"

"To tell the truth, Dr. Rideau," Joe said, "we've been pretty busy on a few other things."

The doctor frowned and put the magnifying glass aside. "You're not too young to think about investing for the future. What did you say your father does?"

"He's a detective," Frank replied.

"Ah—well. I hope he has some investments in the fruit of our mints."

Mrs. Rideau steered the conversation away from her husband's favorite subject.

"Dear, I was telling them about our troubles."

"Oh, yes. The Indians," Dr. Rideau said, pursing his lips thoughtfully.

"Then you found out the prowlers were really Senecas?" Frank asked.

"Of course. They kept shaking their rattles."

"Why would they want to let you know that they were Indians?" Joe asked. "It doesn't seem to make sense, Dr. Rideau."

The man looked at him in astonishment. "Of course they'd want me to know. They're trying to get at my treasure, because they think I have the melted coins."

"Old Spoon Mouth, you mean," Frank said with a smile.

"Spoon Mouth—Moon Face—whatever they call it," the doctor said testily. "I don't have it!"

Remembering the parted curtain upstairs, Joe discreetly asked whether their tenants had heard the prowlers.

"Yes, they did. And they're mighty upset," Mrs. Rideau replied.

Frank took up the questioning. "You say they

are researchers, who also teach in college. Could that be at Zoar College in the summer?"

Mrs. Rideau seemed pleased that the boy's guess had been so accurate. "Why, yes, that's exactly what they do."

Frank took a plunge by asking bluntly, "Do you folks know an Elmont Chidsee?"

There was not a moment's hesitation. "Yes. Of course. He's visiting upstairs right now. I understand he'll stay overnight."

Joe rolled his eyes and said to Frank, "Oh, boy! That spells trouble!"

"Did you say trouble?" Mrs. Rideau asked.

"Yes. We're sorry you had this trouble," Joe said quickly. "But if the police know all about it, I feel that you're safe enough, at least from outside prowlers."

Mrs. Rideau excused herself and went to the kitchen to turn off the stove. The doctor, meanwhile, shuffled downstairs to put his coins away.

Frank and Joe had an opportunity to talk things over. "The Rideaus are very naive not to suspect their tenants," Frank remarked.

"We'll just have to protect them," Joe decided.

The boys laid out a plan, and when Mrs. Rideau returned, Frank said that they would like to sleep in the Rideaus' basement that night.

"That would be fine," she said. "In fact, there's a cot in the old dental office already. We can put another one there."

"But," Joe added, "first we'll go into the barn as if we were planning to spend the night there. Then the prowlers will be thrown off."

"Right," Frank went on. "And if they should happen to break into the house, Joe and I will grab them!"

Mrs. Rideau chuckled and said, "My, you are brave boys. But our dogs would grab the ruffians before you had a chance!"

While supper was being prepared, the Hardys joined the doctor in the basement. He showed them the coin vault and took them to his old dental office, where they would sleep.

"I never sold any of my equipment," he stated proudly, and pointed to the chair, the tools, and his drill. "That's an air drill. Fine instrument. I always bought the best."

The Hardys returned to the dining room, where Mrs. Rideau served a succulent beef stew along with a generous green salad. All the while Frank and Joe listened for sounds from upstairs. If Chidsee was there with the professors, he was keeping mighty quiet.

When darkness came, Frank and Joe took flashlights and their bags and went to the barn. They talked for half an hour, watching the upstairs windows of the Rideau house. Several times figures moved back and forth, but they were too indistinct to be recognized.

Finally Frank said, "Okay, Joe. Ready to go to the dentist?"

"Please, not the air drill!" Joe protested.

They crept through the darkness, opened the back door quietly, and descended into the basement.

"I don't think anyone saw us," Frank said as they stretched out on the cots.

The boys decided to spell each other with guard duty during the night. Frank slept first while Joe watched. At the end of two hours the younger boy roused his brother.

"Your turn," he said. "I didn't hear a sound."

Some time past midnight, Frank was startled by a faint rattling noise, then he heard footsteps coming slowly down the basement stairs. He alerted Joe and gave the high sign for quiet.

Both rose quickly and stood on either side of the door. They could hear the knob being turned.

They held their breath and tensed to spring. The door opened. Frank flicked on the light.

There stood Dr. Rideau!

"All right boys, it's only me," he whispered hoarsely. "You can turn the light off."

"What are you doing here?" Joe asked, irritated by the needless fright.

"I just wanted to see if you fellows were all right."

"But what about that rattling sound we heard?"

"Hm!" The doctor thought for a moment, then put his hands in his bathrobe pocket and jiggled some coins. "I guess this is what caused it."

"I suppose it is," Frank said, yawning. "Well, you'd better get back to sleep, Doctor. We'll take care of things."

Rideau padded up the stairs and the Hardys turned off the light.

"Wow!" Joe said. "Guess I might as well stand watch now. I'm wide awake again."

Frank laid down and closed his eyes, but only for a few moments. From the floor above came a bloodcurdling cry!

CHAPTER XII

Trustworthy Men

FOR the second time that night the Hardys were jolted into action.

"It sounds as if someone's being murdered!" exclaimed Joe as he and Frank took the steps two at a time. When they opened the kitchen door, they heard Mrs. Rideau moaning, "Oh, my poor babies!"

Frank and Joe burst into the living room to see the elderly couple in their bathrobes, kneeling beside the two dogs. Tay and Boots lay on their sides, tongues lolling, and their chests heaving with short rasping breaths.

"What happened?" Frank asked. "What's the matter with the dogs?"

Mrs. Rideau said that after her husband had gone to the basement, Tay and Boots had become restless. "I thought perhaps somebody might be prowling around outside," she said, "so I let them out for a few minutes. When they came back, they acted strangely."

"Do you suppose they ate anything while they were out?" asked Joe.

The Rideaus doubted this. "They've been trained not to take anything unless we give it to them," the doctor explained.

"Well, they're sick, that's for sure," Frank said. "Have you called the vet?"

"Not yet," replied Dr. Rideau. "There's the number on a list beside the phone."

While the doctor comforted his wife, Frank quickly called the veterinarian.

"I'm sorry to bother you this late at night," he said, "but the Rideaus' two dogs are in bad trouble." Frank listened, then he went on, "Yes, we'll bring them over right away."

Dr. Rideau dressed hurriedly and backed the car to the front of the house. Frank and Joe, straining under the weight of the immense beasts, carried the limp forms to the waiting automobile.

"Joe," Frank said, "you stay with Mrs. Rideau. I'll go along. I don't want to leave this place unguarded."

By the time they reached the veterinarian's office, his lights were on. Seeing the car, he hastened outside and helped Frank with the animals, who were now rasping at an even greater rate.

"Poison," the vet muttered. He put Tay on the

table and quickly injected an antidote, and a heart stimulant. Then he did the same for Boots.

"I'll be frank with you," he said to Dr. Rideau. "I don't know if we can save them. But I certainly will give it a good try."

Then he asked questions about the dogs' activities. "You're sure they ate no poisoned food?"

"I'm certain of that."

The vet examined every inch of Tay's body. Near the dog's rump his finger touched something sharp. He looked at it closely and pulled out a tiny needle.

"Here's your answer," he said. "He's been shot by a poison dart!"

Dr. Rideau shook his fist. "Those murdering Indians!" he muttered. "They were prowling around and shot my dogs!"

"We can't be sure they did it," Frank said quietly.

The vet also recovered a miniature missile from Boot's back. Both dogs seemed to be breathing easier now as the medication took effect.

With Frank's help, the vet placed the animals in spotless compartments in a room adjoining his office. Then he went to the phone and reported the incident to the police.

By the time Dr. Rideau and Frank returned to the house, a police car was in front and two officers with powerful flashlights were searching the property. Frank and Joe joined them, but after twenty minutes could not find any evidence of an intruder.

Frank took Joe aside. "Any sign of the profs or our buddy Elmont?"

"They were questioned, but it seems they slept right through the whole thing," Joe replied. "Then they came down in their robes and gave Mrs. Rideau a line of baloney. Took her upstairs to rest!"

"What do they look like?" Frank asked. "Have you ever seen them before?"

Joe shook his head. "No. They're handsome, thirtyish, smooth—too smooth!"

"Did Elmont come down, too?"

"No, luckily he didn't. I wasn't keen on seeing him at all!"

The boys went back to the basement and resumed their watch, but everything was quiet for the rest of the night.

The next morning they talked with the Rideaus before breakfast. "I asked our tenants upstairs to redouble their surveillance of the premises," the doctor stated. "Especially since Tay and Boots are hospitalized."

"Did they say they would?" Frank inquired.

"Oh, yes. They'll keep an eye on the place. I must say, I feel much better about it."

Frank and Joe stepped outside. "What do you know about that!" Frank said. "It's like asking the fox to guard the chicken coop!"

"They're being set up for a robbery," Joe remarked. "Wouldn't you think that he'd see it?"

The boys walked to the barn. There were blankets to be folded and cots put away. When Frank opened the door, he sucked in his breath.

"Good night, Joe! Look at this!"

A bale of hay had fallen from the loft and landed on Frank's cot. The legs were smashed and the fabric ripped.

"And to think you might have been sleeping there!" Joe exclaimed, shuddering.

"Our prowler last night didn't miss a trick," Frank said, shaking his head gravely. "Joe, if thieves are going to strike at Dr. Rideau's treasure, it'll be soon. I feel it in my bones!"

The boys straightened out their blankets and went into the house for breakfast. They decided to withhold the story of the splintered cot, so as not to disturb the couple any further.

Frank, however, felt obliged to tell them about their suspicions. After the meal he pushed his chair back, looked at the Rideaus levelly, and said, "I don't want to upset you nice people, but I think you're going to have a robbery here—and soon!"

"Oh dear!" Mrs. Rideau said. "And we won't have our dogs for protection!"

"That's part of the plan," Joe said. "Getting rid of Tay and Boots eliminates one big obstacle for the thieves."

The woman heaved a sigh and went on, "But at least we have our professors. I don't think anybody would rob this house while they're about."

"In this case, I don't think I'd trust anybody," Frank said.

The doctor put down his coffee cup and smiled benignly. "My, but aren't you suspicious! The professors are educated men, and very trustworthy!"

Just then hastening footsteps were heard on the stairs. The front door opened and closed.

"There they go now," the doctor remarked.

"I've never met them," Frank said.

"Let me show you some snapshots," Mrs. Rideau said eagerly. She went to the living room, opened the drawer of an end table, and returned with an envelope of photos.

"We had a picnic in the yard a couple of weeks ago," she explained, handing the prints to Frank. "Aren't the professors handsome?"

"Yes, they are," Frank said slowly. "And this is a good picture of you and the doctor, too." As he looked over the photographs, he took a snapshot of the professors out of the pile and, unnoticed by the Rideaus, slipped it in his pocket. He would return it later. Then he handed back the rest of the pictures.

"Would you like another glass of milk?" Mrs. Rideau asked.

The boys said No, they had enjoyed a good

breakfast. Everyone got up, and while the Rideaus busied themselves in the kitchen, the Hardys walked quietly up the stairs.

"Maybe we can investigate their apartment," Joe whispered. "You think they're all out?"

Frank nodded. "It sounded like three people leaving. Let's risk it."

Frank tried the door. It was locked. "We can't break in," he said. "And if we picked the lock and were found out—"

"I know what you mean," Joe interrupted. "It would infuriate the Rideaus. The profs have a real in with these people."

The boys trotted down the stairs and sat in the living room, mulling over what to do next. Frank pulled out the snapshot and showed it to Joe.

"Why did you take it?" Joe asked.

"I want to send it to Sam Radley and see if he can give us a rundown on these people, provided, of course, that they have a record."

"Smart thinking!"

The phone rang. Mrs. Rideau picked up the extension in the kitchen, then called out, "It's for the Hardys!"

Frank took the instrument. Chet's voice, agitated and abrupt, came over the wire. "I'm at Niagara Falls. In trouble. Keystone—"

With a click, the phone went dead.

CHAPTER XIII

A Startled Seneca

CHET Morton's abrupt message for help plunged the Hardys into a quandary.

"We're in a real bind," Frank said. "Chet's in Niagara Falls, probably kidnapped, and the coin collection seems ripe for a heist."

"What'll we do?" Joe asked.

"When you come right down to it, there's no choice. Chet's worth more than all the money stashed away downstairs."

However, the young sleuths decided to appeal to the local police. Excusing themselves, they hastened to headquarters.

Frank was careful not to accuse anyone. If the professors were not guilty of any wrongdoing, the Hardys might be subject to slander proceedings. They had to couch their suspicions in the mildest of terms.

They approached the desk sergeant and requested to see the police chief.

"What is your business?" he asked them.

"We have some suspicions," Frank said, "that we would like to report to the chief."

"I can take the complaint."

"It's not a complaint," Joe said. "It's just—"

Having heard the conversation, the chief stepped out of his office. He was a short stout man with a thatch of cropped gray hair. "What can I do for you?" he asked. "My name's White."

The Hardys introduced themselves and asked if they could speak with him privately.

The man ushered them into his office and motioned them to be seated. He settled back in his swivel chair, folded his hands over his midsection, and regarded Frank and Joe with a fixed expression.

"To put it bluntly," Frank began, "we suspect that Dr. Rideau's coin vault may be robbed soon."

"Really?" Chief White seemed unimpressed.

"I wonder if you could give him some protection, for a while, at least," Frank went on.

"How come you're so concerned about this possible theft? If what you say is true, why hasn't Dr. Rideau asked us for protection?"

Frank told of their accidental meeting on the highway; how they had dropped in on the couple and learned about the prowlers; and how Tay and Boots had been knocked out by poison darts.

"We know all about that," White said, putting his elbows on the desk. "Do you think we're asleep at the switch?"

Frank and Joe were quick to deny any such thought.

"Well, that's better. I don't like any young fellows accusing us of inaction."

"Not at all, sir," Frank said. "I'm sure you know about the situation. But there's one thing you don't know." He proceeded to tell the story of the bale of hay which had smashed his cot in the barn.

The chief was thoughtful. "It could have been an accident," he said slowly.

"The mask wasn't," Joe put in, and told of Chet's experience.

"I agree it seems as if someone wants to get you out of the way," Chief White said. "Unfortunately all we have are suspicions without a suspect. Tell you what. I'll have my men patrol the Rideau house more often, especially at night. I can't spare anyone to stand guard around the clock—"

Frank got up. "We realize that, Chief. But I think that will help. We'll have to leave for a few days on an emergency, and when we get back, we'll pitch in, too."

"Okay. Let me know if something else develops." The chief walked the boys to the door, and they said good-by.

On the way back they passed the post office. A public phone booth stood on the corner in front of the building. "I'm going to try to reach Radley," Frank said and stepped inside.

Sam was at his hotel in Cleveland, and before Frank could tell his story, he asked, "Did Chet get there? He started yesterday. The car's all fixed. Looks like new."

When Frank told him about Chet's call, Sam was shocked. "Niagara Falls?" he repeated. "How did he get up there?"

"Our guess is he's been kidnapped," Frank replied. Then he told what had happened at Hawk Head.

Radley immediately questioned the authenticity of the professors.

"I'm putting the picture in the mail to you," Frank said. "Could you check with the FBI?"

"Sure thing. By the way, your dad is in Florida."

"No kidding. Some people have all the luck!"

"Don't envy him. This is no vacation. He's on the trail of that mail fraud gang. It ties in with the bunch of phonies here in Cleveland."

"Dad thought it might," said Frank.

"Listen, what are you going to do about Chet?" Sam asked.

"We're going to Niagara Falls as quickly as possible. The key word is Keystone."

"Tough assignment."

"Don't worry. We'll find him."

After mailing the snapshot taken in the Rideaus' yard, Frank and Joe went back to the house, packed their bags, and told their hosts they had to leave. They urged the doctor and his wife to be very careful, especially without the dogs.

"The vet called and told me that Tay and Boots will be better in a few days," Mrs. Rideau said with a smile.

"I'm glad to hear that," Frank replied and the boys said good-by.

They hopped a bus to Yellow Springs, where they would have to transfer to Niagara Falls. The driver let them off in front of the Sunset Motel.

"Any messages for us?" Joe asked at the desk.

The manager smiled. "I guess you were expecting him." He pointed to a shiny red car parked beside the driveway. The fellow in it was dozing behind the wheel.

"Did he say who he was and what he wanted?" Frank asked, surprised.

"No. But I've seen him around here. By the way, I didn't hear from that Morton fellow."

Frank nodded and they left the office. Quickly they put their bags in their room, then approached the red car. The driver, a dark-haired young man in his twenties, looked like an Indian. His head lolled to one side on the palm of his hand, which rested against the car door.

Frank and Joe stared at him for a few seconds before Frank said, "Hi, there!"

The driver jumped awake, his elbow banging against the horn, which emitted a two-tone blast. Frank and Joe jumped in reaction, then started to laugh, as did the young man who stepped out.

He was wearing khaki trousers and a blue work shirt which stretched tight over his broad shoulders as he offered a handshake. "I'm Paul Jimerson," he said, "and you must be the Hardy boys. My mother gave me a good description of you."

"Rod's brother?" Joe asked.

"That's right."

"We thought you were working in Buffalo," Frank put in.

"I was, but our plant has been shut down for a week. So I came home."

"For your mother's corn soup, I'll bet," Joe quipped.

Paul Jimerson, unlike Lendo Wallace, was a very outgoing person and full of bouncy enthusiasm.

"Hey, what do you think of my new car?" he asked. "Isn't she a beauty?" Then he ran a hand through his hair and looked embarrassed. "I didn't mean to brag. But I just got it a few days ago. He added, "My mother told me about you, and I wonder if there's anything I can do for you."

"You bet," Joe said. "We need a driver!"

"Where do you want to go?"

"Niagara Falls."

The Indian shrugged and grinned. "I'm game for a little sightseeing."

"It's not exactly sightseeing," Frank said. "All we hope to see is our friend." He felt that Paul could be trusted and related the story of Chet's SOS.

"And you expect to find him?" Paul asked. "Niagara Falls is not exactly a little town, you know."

"We know. We've got to follow the Keystone clue," Frank said.

"How about some lunch before we start out?" Joe suggested.

"Good idea." Paul grinned. "I'm hungry."

As they ate their sandwiches, Frank and Joe guardedly discussed the case of the missing Indian masks.

"I don't know too much about it," Paul said, "but Rod is quite upset about the whole business. He's closer to our old Indian customs than I am."

"Look, I have a suggestion," said Joe. "Before we start out, let's talk with Lendo Wallace again. I'd like to ask him why he left that danger note. The answer may give us a clue to Chet's whereabouts."

"Okay, let's go," Paul said. "Your chauffeur is at your service!"

A few minutes later they turned into Wallace's

"This resembles you, Frank," Joe exclaimed

driveway. Paul got out and knocked on the door.

"Nobody home," he reported.

As he went back to the car a neighbor hailed him. "If you're looking for Lendo, he's in the woods!"

"Thanks," Paul said, and turned to Frank and Joe. "I think I know just where he might be. Follow me."

The boys got out of the car and Paul led the way into the woods behind Wallace's lot. "He works here quite often," Paul explained. "There are some nice smooth trees for mask-making."

He shouted Lendo's name a couple of times, but there was no reply. Finally they came to a gloomy area of scarred trees, evidence of Wallace's previous mask-making.

"See here?" Paul said, pointing to fresh cuts in a basswood. "He's making a life mask."

All three walked up close and studied it.

"Holy Toledo!" Joe exclaimed. "This resembles you, Frank!"

Paul scanned Frank's face, then the mask. "He's right," he said, a troubled look coming over his face. "I don't like to tell you this, but Lendo regards you as an evil spirit. He's trying to get rid of you, Frank!"

"Do you take this seriously, Paul?" Joe inquired.

Instead of replying, the Indian frowned,

turned, and started to walk out of the woods. The Hardys followed. Finally Paul spoke.

"I do consider this serious, fellows. Why don't you take Lendo's advice and go home?"

Frank and Joe did not reply. When they emerged from the woods, Frank asked, "Are you still going to take us to Niagara Falls?"

"You can back out of it if you want," Joe added.

Paul Jimerson stopped and turned to the boys. His carefree look was back and he grinned. "Of course I'll take you. An Indian doesn't quit, either."

"Good," Joe said. "Now we'll relieve our kidnapping friends of a hungry mouth."

Suddenly Frank bent over and rubbed his leg. "I've been stung by a bee!" he declared. He continued walking for a few minutes, then keeled over, flat on his face!

CHAPTER XIV

Hot on the Trail

AFTER hitting the ground Frank lay still. Joe and Paul quickly rushed to his aid and rolled him over on his back. He looked pale and his breathing was labored.

Joe had read about allergic reaction to bee stings. For some people, it could be fatal. He bared his brother's leg to examine the spot.

"Good night!" he cried out. "Paul, look at this!"

A miniature dart had punctured the skin. Joe pulled it out. "Frank's in great danger!" he said anxiously. "He's been shot like Dr. Rideau's dogs. We must get him to a doctor immediately!"

Paul swung the injured boy on his back and hurried to the car. Joe glanced around for a suspect. There was no one in sight.

"I'll bet it was Lendo Wallace," he said

through clenched teeth as they laid Frank on the back seat.

"I think you're wrong. Lendo wouldn't do a thing like that!" Paul replied. "Anyway, I know a doctor who has his office not far from here. I'll take you there."

They sped to the address, five miles distant. The physician was just leaving when Joe intercepted him at the door.

"My brother's been shot by a poison dart!" he said. "You must help him!"

"Where is he? Bring him right in here," the doctor ordered.

Paul carried Frank inside, put him on an examining table, and after a quick analysis of the poison missile, the doctor administered an antidote.

"Good thing you brought him here fast," he said, after observing Frank's reaction for a while. "He's out of danger now. He should stay at the hospital overnight, though."

Frank had regained consciousness. When he heard the doctor's words, he said feebly, "I can't do that. We have urgent business in Niagara Falls."

The physician turned to Joe. "Now look. Your brother is not well and can't do anything strenuous. He needs rest!"

"I'll see to it that he gets it," Joe assured him. "We'll take him with us and as soon as we get there he'll go to bed."

Paul and Joe helped Frank into the car.

"All set for the honeymoon center?" Paul asked Joe.

"Right. Do you know a place there where we can stay?"

"I've got a cousin. His kids are in college. Maybe we can sleep there."

"Great. One more thing. We'd better report this incident to the police."

They stopped at headquarters and Joe related the details of the dart assault. He told the chief where they were going, saying they expected to be back at the Sunset Motel in a day or two.

The chief promised to have the wooded area searched for clues, and the boys left.

The trip to Niagara Falls was uneventful. Paul drove directly to the home of his cousin. The man, who was considerably older, made wrought-iron furniture and had his own shop.

His wife, a plump, cordial woman, invited them to stay as long as they wished. She led Frank and Joe to one room and Paul to another. "Now that the children are gone, we have plenty of extra space," she said with a smile.

After supper Frank went directly to bed, while Joe phoned the Rideaus. The doctor answered and told him that Tay and Boots were still at the vet's, but recovering nicely. Joe did not mention the poison dart, because he saw no reason to alarm the man. He did, however, caution him once more and urged the tightest security on his coin vault.

Later in the evening Joe and Paul pored over the Niagara Falls telephone book and directories, looking for the name Keystone.

The yellow pages of the classified directory revealed no hotel or motel by that name. "But look here," Joe said. "There's a delicatessen and an auto supply store. Let's check them out in the morning."

He and Paul had a hearty breakfast after a good night's rest, but Frank did not feel like eating. Their hostess gave him some milk and he went back to bed.

The auto supply store was the first stop for Paul and Joe. They parked in front, went inside, and looked around at the usual myriad of accessories.

A clerk approached them. "Can I help you?"

"Maybe. I'm looking for a fellow named Chet Morton. He might have come in here yesterday."

"What did he look like?"

Joe described Chet in detail.

"Fat guys walk into the store all the time," the clerk said. "But I don't remember that one."

Joe strolled about with Paul, speaking in a loud voice and mentioning the name Bayport. If Chet was near, he certainly would hear them.

The clerk became annoyed. "You guys don't have to shout. And what's all this bit about Bayport?"

Joe pointed to Paul. "He can't hear too well."

"All right. But what do you want? Window-shopping is for the women."

Joe was embarrassed. He walked over to a stack of automobile mats, picked up one, and said, "We'll take this."

The clerk wrapped it, Joe paid, and they left.

"That was a dud," Paul said. "Where to now?"

"The delicatessen. Chet would be hard to get out of that—if he was ever in there. He loves to eat."

The Keystone Delicatessen was downtown. The boys entered and Joe made the same inquiries. The fellow behind the counter, a stout, bald-headed man in a white apron, had not heard of Chet Morton. And he had not made a cream cheese and salami sandwich for any customer.

Just then a clerk at the other end of the counter spoke up. "I made one for somebody yesterday!"

"Was he a boy about my age?" asked Joe.

"No. He was at least fifty."

Joe thanked him and they walked out. "Another lead blown," he grumbled. "The Keystone-whatever-it-is can't be very big, because it's not advertised."

"Maybe Chet said something else and you got it wrong," Paul suggested.

Joe shook his head. "No. It was Keystone. And we'll just have to work on that clue until we find Chet."

'I think we'll do better on foot," said Paul.

"That way I don't have to watch traffic—we can both look."

Joe agreed and they parked the car. They wandered in and out of the downtown streets, pausing only briefly for lunch. The afternoon grew hot and the sun sent its glaring rays over the busy sidewalks.

Finally they rounded a corner, not far from their parking spot. Joe stopped in his tracks. A small sign over the sidewalk bore the legend KEY-STONE MUSEUM.

Paul looked at the dilapidated storefront. "Oh, man," he said, wriggling his sore toes, "could this really be the fruit of our toil?"

"There's one way to find out," Joe replied. "Let's have a look inside."

He went through the open doorway into the dimly lighted curio museum. Half blinded by the sudden change of light, he nearly ran into the ticket seller, a tall gangly man standing beside a pedestal.

"Sorry," Joe said. "I couldn't see. How much is the admission?"

"One dollar a piece."

"Boy, that's steep!" said Joe. "What have you got in here? The crown jewels?"

Stony-faced, the attendant rattled off a list of the exhibits: photographs of daring deeds at the Falls; barrels which had survived the trip over the brink; wax figures of the men who risked their lives in various stunts, notably the famous Blondin crossing over the cataract on a wire. "We also have a few old whale ribs," he concluded, smoothing his gray hair.

"From the Falls?" Joe asked innocently.

"Are you trying to be funny?"

"Sorry, Mr.—"

"Janzig. Not that it would mean anything to you."

"Well, thank you, Mr. Janzig. We'll take two tickets."

The man grabbed the two dollars. "Look all you want," he said with a supercilious smile.

Up to now, Paul had been silent. Once they were out of earshot, he said, "I don't like that character. He rubbed me the wrong way."

"Same here," Joe replied, glancing around the room. "What a lot of junk."

Faded pictures in ornate frames showed people of bygone years standing above the famous cataract. Joe doubted the authenticity of the broken barrels which were supposed to have carried adventurers over the brink.

Looking around, he moved toward a door at the back of the museum. He turned the knob and peered inside. The musty-smelling room was piled high with things that had obviously been discarded from the museum.

Joe closed the door quietly and turned to Paul. "I'd like to sneak in there. Can you—?"

As he spoke, Janzig appeared out of nowhere. "What are you doing?" he demanded.

"Just looking around," Joe replied.

"That back room is not part of the museum."

"You got something to hide?"

"Oh, a fresh kid!" Janzig gave Joe a hard look. Just then a deep voice barked, "Hey!"

The boys turned to see a burly man with dark hair standing in the open doorway to the museum.

"How about some service?" he rumbled.

Looking startled, Janzig swallowed nervously. "Right away, sir," he said, and hastened to the front.

"Now, quick!" Joe whispered. He opened the door and slipped into the back room with Paul behind him. The Indian closed the door softly.

"Chet!" he called. "Chet, where are you?"

"Chet, are you in here?" Joe ran to the far side of the room.

From somewhere came a muffled cry!

CHAPTER XV

On the Brink

"CHET, answer me!" Joe called out.

The sound of a scuffle seemed to come from a pile of boxes which stood one atop the other, nearly reaching the ceiling. Joe shouldered them aside, and as they came crashing to the floor, he saw a door behind them. He tried it. "Locked," he said.

He and Paul crashed against it, forcing the lock. With a bang the door flung open, revealing another storage room much like the first. On the far side a door was ajar. As Joe raced for it, he saw through a dirty window that somebody was being hustled into a small, black, unmarked truck.

"Stop!" Joe shouted. As he reached for the doorknob, someone on the other side gave a hard kick, knocking Joe backward into Paul. The two fell to the floor, and by the time they scrambled to their feet, the truck was roaring away.

The boys raced into the alley, but the vehicle had vanished.

"Do you think they have your friend Chet?" asked Paul when they turned back inside.

"I'm sure they do," Joe replied. "But I'll have to find proof."

Janzig, by now, had hurried into the back room. "What's going on here?" he demanded.

"Where's Chet Morton?" Joe glared at him angrily.

"I don't know what you're talking about." Janzig put a cigarette to his lips and lighted it. Joe noticed that his hand shook.

"Didn't you know someone was in that back room?" Paul spoke up.

Janzig dragged hard on the cigarette, coughed, and shook his head. "I don't know anything about anybody in the back. It's a storage place, that's all. Now look. I want no trouble. Why don't you go away?"

"We're going to search the place first!"

"Go ahead. Be my guest!"

Joe turned to Paul. "You stay here and keep an eye on him. I'll check the back."

Empty boxes and assorted junk and piles of magazines cluttered the dusty room. A telephone was mounted on the wall near the door. Joe rummaged around, looking for clues. If only he could find some evidence that it was really Chet who had been there!

He turned boxes over and studied every scrap of paper on the floor, but found nothing of importance. Suddenly a thought occurred to him. Maybe something had been dropped in the struggle outside!

He opened the door and glanced about the alley. His eyes lit upon a small white paper bag near the side of the building. Joe seized it, opened it, and pulled out a plastic wrapper. Inside was half a cream cheese and salami sandwich!

"It must be Chet's!" Joe thought. Now he had evidence! He slipped the bag into his pocket so Janzig would not see it. Then he made his way through the clutter back into the museum, where Paul and Janzig were having a glaring match.

"You didn't find anything. I told you you wouldn't!" the attendant said.

Joe managed a smile. "I guess you were right. I got all worked up about nothing."

Paul looked at Joe in disbelief. How come this sudden turnabout? Joe threw him a quick wink, turned to the ticket seller again, and said, "Nobody's perfect. We all make mistakes. Will you accept my apology?"

Janzig tossed his cigarette to the floor, snubbed it out with his foot, and with a pleased look said, "Yeah, yeah, I know. I was young once myself. No hard feelings."

The boys strolled out to the sidewalk, down the

street, and turned the corner which led to the alley.

"What happened to you?" asked Paul. "One minute you're like a tiger, then you turn into a pussycat."

"Paul, Chet was really there! He's the one they took away in the black truck!"

"Are you sure?"

Joe produced the cream cheese and salami sandwich. He theorized that Chet had been held in the back room, and being hungry, had asked for his favorite snack.

"And Janzig probably was the guy who bought it at the deli!"

"Right. Now follow me and be very quiet."

Keeping close to the wall, Joe made his way quickly to the window of the rear room. He peered through the smudged glass. His hunch was correct. Standing with his back toward the boys, Janzig dialed the phone.

Joe listened intently, glad that the window was open a crack at the bottom. In a low voice the attendant said only two words "They're here!" Then he hung up.

The young sleuth backed off, motioning to Paul. "Come on. We have to find that truck!" he said.

They were up against a gang of hoods, Joe realized, much more sinister than he had imagined.

Chet was being held as a hostage. Now their enemies had been alerted that the Hardys were hot on their trail in Niagara Falls!

The two ran to the car and drove around block by block, looking for the unmarked truck. But no luck!

Finally Joe said, "Paul, let's stop in and see how Frank is. Besides, I want to tell him what's going on."

Frank was sitting up in bed, still weak, but gaining strength rapidly. Their kind hostess had made him a strong broth which he sipped as Joe quickly related what had occurred at the museum.

Frank nearly dropped the cup of broth. "Good night, Joe! We've got to work fast!" He put down the nearly finished broth, swung out of bed, and grabbed his clothes.

"Listen, Frank. You're not well enough yet," Joe objected.

"I'm going!" was the determined answer. "You ready for the hunt, Paul?"

The Indian grinned and followed the boys outside to his car. Perspiration stood out on Frank's brow and Joe noticed it. "Are you sure you're okay?" he asked.

"Getting better every second," his brother replied firmly.

As the car pulled away from the curb, Frank said, "My advice is to go back to that alley. Maybe we'll find another clue."

The Indian guided the car with the skill of a racing veteran. Approaching their destination, he eased the brakes and poked the vehicle slowly around the corner.

Joe sucked in his breath. "Frank! There it is! The same truck!"

The elbow of the driver could be seen protruding through the cab window. Just then Janzig hastened through the rear door, got into the front seat, glanced back and noticed Paul's car. He gave a cry of alarm and the truck was off!

"We've got to get them!" Joe said. "I'll bet Chet is still in there!"

"Good grief!" said Paul. "I wonder where they're taking him."

"We'll find out," Frank said. "Cut him off if you can, Paul."

The twisting, turning chase led through the heart of the city. The truck passed a red light, and Paul, afraid that they would lose their quarry, eased through the intersection with horn blaring.

A policeman on the corner waved his arms frantically and blew his whistle. He put his walkie-talkie to his lips.

"That's all we need!" muttered Joe, who had watched him. "I hope they don't stop us before we catch that truck!"

They neared the park by the side of the Falls, where a slow car in front of the truck cut down its speed. "Get him, Paul. Get him now!" Joe urged.

The Indian deftly made a right turn, neatly cutting off the truck. It jumped the curb, ran across the narrow park, and hit a tree not far from the churning rapids.

The boys leaped from their car and reached the truck just as the driver and Janzig hopped out the front. Then the back opened up for a second. A big burly fellow jumped out, slammed the door, and came at the boys, his huge fists flailing.

Paul took him on while Joe sailed into the driver. This left Frank to combat Janzig. The fellow, though thin, was wiry. He feinted a left to the head, then whacked Frank on the right side of the jaw.

Weak from the dart poison, Frank reeled back, crashing into the guard rail which protected onlookers from the precipitous drop into the roaring waters of Niagara Falls.

Joe and Paul were having their troubles, too. Their opponents kicked, gouged, elbowed, and fought a hard, mean battle.

Paul turned to help Frank, but the moment he did, the thugs leaped upon them and the four went crashing to the pavement.

"Stop! Don't do it!" Joe cried out as Janzig did his best to lift Frank up and over the rail. The weakened boy clung to the metal top rail piping with all his might. The world went swimming around.

Frank drew his knees back, lashed out with his

feet, and caught his attacker in the chest. Janzig groaned and fell to his knees. But the impetus of Frank's thrust catapulted the boy to the far side of the railing.

With a supreme effort Joe dealt his foe a sharp karate chop, then leaped for the railing. He got a scissors hold around Frank and pulled him back to safety.

By this time a crowd had gathered. A car screeched to a halt and two young men dashed through it and pitched into the fray. Out of the corner of his eye, Joe recognized Biff Hooper and Tony Prito! He must be dreaming! What were they doing here?

A flurry of well-aimed blows from Joe sent the driver reeling, and Paul put away the big thug with a sledge-hammer blow to the side of his face.

Just then sirens sounded. Two police cars pulled up and a group of officers jumped out. "Break it up! Break it up!" a sergeant shouted.

"They're broken up all right!" Biff replied as the police ran up.

The trio, sprawled on the ground, rose shakily to their feet.

"These men are kidnappers!" Joe charged.

"What do you mean?" Janzig said. "We were just driving along when these guys cut us off and attacked us!" He glared balefully at Biff and Tony, who had turned the tide of the battle.

"Who are you?" the sergeant asked.

The Bayport reinforcement duo introduced themselves and said they were on their way to the Upper Michigan peninsula to do some fishing.

"Mr. Radley, a friend of ours, alerted us that our buddies here might be in trouble in Niagara Falls," Tony explained. "So we stopped by and helped."

Frank and Joe identified themselves, as did Paul. The beaten men, still rubbing their jaws, gave their names too.

"You say they're kidnappers?" the officer asked Joe. "Whom did they kidnap?"

"Chet Morton from Bayport," Frank put in. "He's in that black truck!" He pointed to the vehicle.

The policeman walked over and flung open the back doors. *The truck was empty!*

"What did I tell you?" Janzig said jubilantly. "These kids are fakes!"

The Hardys and their companions were in a tight predicament. How could they prove their story? And what had happened to Chet? Where had he vanished?

"And what's more," Janzig went on, "I prefer charges against these punks for assault and battery!"

Joe felt as if he had turned to lead. The spinning inside Frank's head grew unbearable, and Paul looked around helplessly.

"Okay, down to headquarters with you!" the

sergeant said sharply, and his men started to lead the boys toward the police cars.

"Wait a minute!" Paul said.

"For what?" the officer behind him asked impatiently.

"Listen!" Above the sound of the traffic and the chatter of the excited onlookers, a sound came from the direction of the truck.

Paul moved over with the policeman on his heels and listened closely. "Somebody is in there, I'll bet!" he exclaimed.

The sergeant climbed inside the truck.

Another officer crawled beneath it.

"Hey! There's a false bottom here!" the sergeant called out after a few seconds. He found a panel and pulled it up.

Underneath, squeezed into a narrow space, was Chet Morton!

CHAPTER XVI

Thieves Strike Twice

TAKING the stout boy's arms, the officer pulled him from the small space where he was wedged under the floor.

Chet looked about, unbelieving at first. "Hi, fellows," he said with a weak wave of the hand as two policemen helped him out of the black truck. Seeing that he was the central figure in the drama, Chet recovered quickly.

Color came into his pale cheeks. He stood erect and pointed an accusing finger at his abductors. "I charge them with kidnapping!" he declared in a firm voice.

Handcuffs were snapped on the trio and the police herded them into one of the patrol cars. With sirens wailing, they were whisked off while Chet related the high points of his adventure.

"I was waylaid," he explained, "soon after I got the car out of the repair shop. Three men cut me off. Creepy and another guy jumped out of the

car, put a gun on me, and forced me into the back
seat of the convertible. Then they took off with
it."

"Didn't anybody see it happen?" asked Frank.

"I don't know. It only took a minute," Chet
replied.

The kidnappers had driven him directly to Niagara Falls and had hidden him in the rear of the
museum. "I got loose and phoned you once,"
Chet said. "They discovered what I was doing and
really belted me!"

The crowd had now dispersed and Joe introduced their Bayport pals to Paul.

"You guys came on strong," the Indian said
with a grin. "How did you find us?"

"Sam Radley gave us the Keystone clue," Tony
explained. "We were cruising around looking for
the place when we spotted you tearing through
town after the truck."

"It took us a while to catch up," Biff added,
"but traffic was heavy."

The police requested the boys to come down to
headquarters to make their complaint. There the
Hardys continued to question Chet. He con-
firmed Frank's belief that the gang were involved
in big crime operations.

"You're in their hair," said Chet and added, "I
heard them mention your father."

Frank and Joe registered surprise. "In what
way?" Joe asked.

"Remember when Rod Jimerson got bopped at the motel in Cleveland?"

Frank and Joe nodded while the police stenographer continued to make notes.

"Well, they thought he was your father for some reason."

"I wonder what—" Joe began.

Frank interrupted by asking the police whether they had come across the Hardys' car and gave them the license number. The chief put the query on intercom and soon the answer squawked out.

The convertible had been found abandoned. It would be returned to the boys if they would come to the police garage.

A short time later the six were dismissed. They thanked the officers for their help and promised to be on hand for the trial of the three kidnappers.

Outside headquarters, Chet made a wry face and said, "Boy, I'm hungry. I could eat a horse!"

"No need for that," Joe quipped. "Here's the lunch you left behind!" With that he pulled the cream cheese and salami sandwich from his pocket and handed it to the astounded Chet.

"Holy Toledo! I dropped that when they pushed me into the truck!" Chet said and wolfed down the food.

They drove to the police garage and claimed the convertible. A quick examination showed it was undamaged.

Frank suggested they all go to Paul's cousin's

house. Biff and Tony followed in Biff's car. When they arrived, they found a snack prepared for them.

"Boy, this sandwich hits the spot!" Frank said.

"Well, I guess we'd better be on our way," Biff declared when he had finished. "Some speckled beauties are waiting for us in those Michigan lakes."

"I'm ready," Tony spoke up. "That is, if you fellows don't need us any longer."

"Go right ahead," Frank said. "And thanks for coming along at the right time. Those goons might have thrown us into the drink if you hadn't."

"It was a great pleasure to take care of them," Biff said with a grin. "Nice to meet you, Paul." They all shook hands, then the two left.

"I'd like to stick around with you for a while, fellows," Paul decided. "I go for this detective work!"

"You're welcome to stay with us," Frank said, then brought the conversation to the missing masks again.

"You know," Paul said, shaking his head, "my brother Rod thinks Lendo Wallace is involved somehow in this. But I don't agree with him."

"Why not?" Frank asked.

Paul said that Lendo had always been an honest person. "When I was a boy, he was awful good to me," he added, and told that many times Lendo had taken him for walks in the woods and had taught him how to throw the snow snake.

"You say you'd like to be a detective," Frank said. "Will you help us to get to the bottom of this mask mystery?"

Paul was enthusiastic over the opportunity. "Let's get started right away," he said.

First, however, Frank put in a call to Radley in Cleveland. He was out, but had given an alternate number where Frank reached him.

"We found Chet," Frank reported. "Thanks for sending the back-up troops!"

Radley was relieved when he heard the story that Chet was safe. "I've received the photo," he said when Frank had finished, "and routed it through the FBI. There's no report on it yet."

"What about the Cadillac?" Frank inquired.

"That wasn't hard to trace. It's owned by John Snedecker."

"No kidding!" Frank exclaimed. "So he's the rich uncle of Elmont Chidsee!"

They chatted a while longer, and Radley said that the Magnitude Merchandising Mart was under close investigation by Mr. Hardy.

"They know Dad's on the case," Frank said. "Rod Jimerson got a bump on the head by being mistaken for him. By the way, how is Rod?"

"Working. No trouble here."

"We're going to the Rideaus' place tomorrow and will stop by the reservation on the way."

"Good luck!" Radley said and hung up.

Next morning Frank rode with Paul to keep him company, while Chet went with Joe in the convertible. Once out of the city traffic, the miles flew by and they soon found themselves nearing Yellow Springs.

Paul, who was in the lead, pulled over to the side of the road and Joe stopped behind him. "Let's drop in on my mother first," Paul suggested.

"Great!" Chet remarked. "I hope she's got some corn soup on the back burner."

The two cars turned into the lane in front of Mrs. Jimerson's home. Before they had a chance to reach the door, the woman approached them. The look of pleasure on her face soon gave way to agitation, however. "Did you come back on account of Lendo Wallace?" she asked.

"No. What happened?" Paul frowned.

"Come on in, and I'll tell you."

In the living room she hugged her son and motioned the callers to sit down. She cast a sidewise glance at Chet and hastened into the kitchen. Shortly she returned with steaming bowls of corn soup.

As the boys ate, she related the story about Wallace. "He was robbed last night. But not only that, he was severely beaten!"

"Robbed?" asked Frank. "What was stolen?"

The woman ticked off the items on her fingers.

"Lacrosse sticks, snow snakes, trinkets, and false faces."

The Hardys were puzzled over the beating.

"Did Lendo come upon the thieves and catch them red-handed, ransacking his house?" Frank asked.

"I don't know," Mrs. Jimerson stated. "The police are investigating."

"It sounds like more than a plain burglary," Paul said grimly. "I'd like to get my hands on his attacker!"

Angrily he rose from the table and put an arm about his mother's shoulders. "Ma, is Lendo home?"

"Yes. But the doctor says he's hurt pretty bad."

"Come on, fellows. Let's go see him!" Paul decided.

Frank, Joe, and Chet finished their soup, thanked Mrs. Jimerson, and hastened out with Paul. They all climbed into his car and drove to Wallace's place.

Paul pushed open the screen door and they entered. The room, obviously a workshop, was in disarray. The door to the bedroom was ajar. Paul entered and beckoned the boys to follow. Lying on the bed with a wide bandage around his head was Lendo Wallace. One purpled eye was closed shut and his face showed other bruises.

The injured man looked feverishly at Paul,

who pulled up a chair and sat close to the bedside.
"Who did this to you, Lendo?" he asked.

"A hundred," Wallace muttered.

"A hundred what?"

The man did not answer, and his friend repeated the question.

"Masks," Lendo whispered finally.

"He's too sick to speak," said Frank. "Maybe we can come back later."

The four left and got into the car before anyone spoke. Then Frank said, "A hundred masks—what does that mean?"

"Don't know," said Joe, "but we'd better find out."

They returned to Mrs. Jimerson and picked up the convertible. This time Chet rode with Paul and the Hardys stayed together. On the way to Hawk Head, Joe flicked on the radio and picked up a local news broadcast. The announcer sounded excited.

"Dr. Rideau's coin vault was robbed last night of more than two hundred thousand dollars in valuable coins," he said. "Local police have no clues to the thieves. They—"

Joe turned off the radio. "They did it!" he exclaimed hotly. "Pour it on, Frank!"

The car gathered speed in the race to Hawk Head.

CHAPTER XVII

A Telltale Cobweb

WHEN Frank reached the city limits of Hawk Head, he slowed down and motioned for Paul to come alongside. He told him of the radio report, then proceeded to the Rideau property.

A police car was at the curb in front of the house, and the chief and a lieutenant stood on the lawn discussing the case.

"Hi, Frank, Joe," Chief White greeted them. "You fellows called the shot that time."

The chief said he had several men inside dusting for fingerprints and making a search of every square inch of the Rideaus' home.

"What time did it happen?" Frank asked.

"Don't know. As you suggested, our patrol car passed the house every half hour during the night."

"And saw nothing suspicious?" Joe asked.

"Not a thing. All was quiet, or so it seemed."

"And the Rideaus," Frank queried, "didn't hear any noises?"

"They were out of town, visiting friends," the police officer replied.

"What?" Joe was incredulous. "They left their coins unguarded?"

"The tenants were home," the chief replied. "Of course the dogs are still at the vet's."

"Have you questioned the professors?" asked Paul.

"Certainly," the chief replied. "We quizzed them first thing." Paul was told that the two men had heard noises briefly. They had come down to check, but found nothing suspicious. "In fact," Chief White said, "they suspect that the Indians did it."

"Were they at home all night?" Frank asked.

"Correct. They never left the place."

Frank noticed the clenched muscles in Paul's jaw. "What makes them think the Indians pulled the job?" he snapped.

The chief put a hand in his pocket and pulled out a small mask. He held it up for Paul to see. "One of the profs found this near the back door when we were making the search."

"That doesn't prove a thing!" Paul protested bitterly.

Frank touched his arm. "Easy does it, Paul. We'll get to the bottom of this!"

Just then Mrs. Rideau, having heard the boys'

voices, hastened from the house. She wrung her hands in agitation as she approached the Hardys. "We should have listened to you!" she kept repeating. "We should have hired a private policeman to stand guard at all times!"

"How's the doctor?" Joe asked.

Mrs. Rideau said he was under sedation, lying on the sofa in the living room. "Our entire fortune is gone. It's all gone!" she wailed.

"How did the thieves get into the vault?" Frank asked.

"It was pretty smooth," White replied. "They used Dr. Rideau's air drill to cut the locks. That way they didn't have to carry any heavy equipment into the house."

"What about fingerprints?" Chet asked.

"Negative. So far at least. Nobody's prints except Dr. Rideau's."

Frank had to admit it was a clever scheme, but carrying off the heavy sacks of coins was another matter. "I have a hunch that the stuff is hidden right around here."

"But we've searched everywhere," Chief White said.

The Hardys, Chet, and Paul excused themselves and went into the house to see Dr. Rideau. He lay pale and still, shocked by the loss of his fortune built up during his long life.

Chet and Paul looked on sympathetically as Frank and Joe questioned Dr. Rideau. But he only repeated what he had already told the police. "The Indians must have done it," he insisted. "They think I have Spoon Mouth!"

"Don't worry, Doctor, your coins will be found," Frank assured him. "Just be patient. We're bound to come upon a clue somewhere!"

Paul grimly held his silence. He beckoned the boys outside and whispered, "That guy is crazy. The Indians wouldn't take his coins. And if they did, what could they do with them?"

"Once a rumor gets started," Frank said, "it's hard to stop it. Somebody must have planted this one intentionally to build up a case against the Senecas."

Frank walked up to Mrs. Rideau, who had just come outside. "By the way, was Elmont Chidsee in the house when it happened?"

"No. Only the professors," she replied.

The Hardys exchanged glances. Was Elmont in on the whole thing or wasn't he?

The four boys put their heads together. "I have a feeling that the loot is hidden in the barn," Joe said. "Remember all that funny business going on there? Maybe the thieves were trying to scare us away for good."

Chet nodded. "Let's check it out."

They walked quietly around the house, opened the barn door, and began to search. Not a shred of evidence was found.

Joe noticed a stubby broom and began to sweep away the straw near the place where Chet had slept. Maybe the stolen coins were underneath it.

"What are you doing?" the stout boy asked, walking over to him.

Crack! Crash!

Rotten floorboards gave away under their combined weight. The two landed hard on the earthen floor of an underground room!

Frank and Paul ran over and peered into the hole. "You went right through an old trap door!" Frank exclaimed. "I can see the outline now!"

"This might be the answer," Joe said, "as to how the intruder got away after putting the mask on Chet." He turned and called to Frank, "Pass me a flashlight, will you?"

Frank ran to the car and returned with a powerful light which he handed down to Joe. While the two boys above watched, Joe and Chet examined the pit carefully.

"Looks like an old root cellar to me," Joe declared.

"Pretty spooky place," Chet said. "I want to get out of here!"

"Oh, oh, Frank! Look at this!" Joe called out.

"Did you find something?"

"Someone has been down here recently." Joe's light shone on a cobweb deep in a corner of the cellar. The symmetry of the fine strands had been broken. Then, on hands and knees, he and Chet

The rotten floorboards gave way

made out the faint outlines of footprints on the dank floor.

"Maybe there's an underground way out of this place!" Paul suggested.

Their sleuthing was suddenly interrupted by Chief White's excited call from outside. "Frank and Joe Hardy!"

Paul and Frank pulled the other two from the root cellar and they hastened out of the barn. The chief beckoned from the house, and the boys ran over to him.

"What's up?" Frank asked.

"We found the melted coins!"

"You mean Spoon Mouth?" Paul asked.

"That's right."

"Where was it?"

"In the back of Mrs. Rideau's closet!"

CHAPTER XVIII

Smashed Evidence

EVERYONE was aghast over the discovery made by the Hawk Head police. Frank and Joe could not believe that the dentist had stolen the melted coins from the Senecas.

Paul Jimerson shook his head sadly. "There's no telling what a man will do to get something he really wants," he said. "But I still feel sorry for the old man."

They all entered the living room to witness a strange scene. The doctor sat on the sofa, his head in his hands. His wife was daubing her eyes with a handkerchief while the chief stood over her, holding the melted coins.

The two professors, meanwhile, had come downstairs. They were upbraiding the elderly couple. Mockton lectured them in his oily sonorous voice, and Glade, looking holier-than-thou, waggled his finger at Mrs. Rideau.

"What harm did the Indians ever do to you?" Glade asked. "Didn't you know Old Spoon Mouth holds a special place in the life of their councils?"

"Stop it!" Dr. Rideau said and looked up pleadingly to the police chief. "I didn't do it! My wife didn't do it, either!"

"Then I suppose Spoon Mouth just walked into Mrs. Rideau's closet," Professor Mockton said. "I must say I didn't realize it was all that valuable as a collector's item."

"It's not!" Dr. Rideau exclaimed. "How could I expect to get rid of it anyway? It's stolen goods!"

"You collectors have ways of doing things. You're all in cahoots. All over the world!"

"Lay off, will you!" Chet growled. Like the Hardys, he hated to see the old couple being badgered.

Although Paul Jimerson was happy that his tribe's heirloom had been recovered, he, too, felt sorry for them.

"Have the Rideaus been advised of their rights?" he asked.

"Yes," Chief White replied.

"I don't want any lawyer," the doctor declared. "I'm not guilty of anything!"

"Well," Mockton said stiffly to the boys, "if you're so concerned about these criminals, that's okay. But we're moving out of this house!"

He went to the telephone, called a drive-it-yourself service, and asked for the use of a small truck. "We'll be there shortly," he said and hung up. Then he and his roommate strode out to their car and drove off.

"I'm afraid you'll have to come down to head-quarters with us," Chief White said to the Rideaus.

They looked shocked and Frank spoke up quickly. "Chief, I just can't believe that these people are guilty."

The officer looked pained. "Neither can I!"

"They've been framed, I'll bet," Joe put in.

Frank requested the police to wait a little while before booking the couple. "Give us a few days and I feel sure we can get to the truth of the matter. The Rideaus won't run away."

"Of course we won't," the doctor spoke up. "I give you my word."

The chief nodded. "Well, Henry, your word's been good in this town for the last thirty years. I guess we can take it for a few more days."

The Rideaus smiled in relief and thanked the officer and the boys. When the police had gone, they retired to their bedroom to rest.

Paul took the opportunity to telephone his brother Rod in Cleveland. He was not at home, but his landlady took the message. Paul told her to have Rod return immediately, so that the Indians could claim Spoon Mouth. "I'll meet him at our mother's house," he said and hung up.

By the time they were all ready to leave for

Yellow Springs, Mockton pulled up into the driveway with a small panel truck, marked U-Drive. Glade followed in their car.

"We're going to get out of here just as soon as we can," Mockton told the boys. "And my advice to you is this: have nothing to do with the Rideaus."

"They were pretty nice to you," Joe said tartly.

"That's right," Frank added. "You seemed to turn on them in an awful hurry."

"You understand," Glade said, mounting the front porch, "that we must protect our professional reputation."

"Big deal," Chet muttered as the professors disappeared into the house.

When Paul and the three boys arrived at Mrs. Jimerson's place, the Indian woman insisted that they remain overnight. Paul broke out some sleeping bags and the tired young sleuths slept comfortable and deeply.

At midmorning a car pulled into the driveway, throwing up dust as the driver stopped short. Rod Jimerson jumped out, trotted to the front of the door, and entered.

"Hi, Mother. Hi, fellows!" he said. "I hear you found old Spoon Mouth!"

"Not us," Frank replied. "The police did."

When Rod was told all that had happened, he shook his head and looked sheepishly at the Hardys. "I was wrong about the whole deal. And I had been so positive, too. I guess I owe Lendo Wallace an apology."

"Poor Lendo," Chet spoke up. "He took a terrible beating."

"And you know something?" Joe said. "That could hardly have been done by Dr. Rideau. We're not to the bottom of this case yet!"

The Jimerson brothers talked quietly about what to do next. It was agreed that Rod should call a meeting of all members of the False Face Society. "We'll form a delegation," he said, "go to the police in Hawk Head, and claim Old Spoon Mouth!"

His mother beamed at the suggestion. "We'll hold a ceremony and celebrate!" she said.

Frank, Joe, and Chet joined the two Senecas as they set out in the Hardys' car to round up members of the society. Lendo Wallace was still too weak to attend.

Early in the afternoon six Indians of the False Face Society met at the Jimerson place. The Bayport boys joined the caravan of three cars which drove to Hawk Head and parked near police headquarters. Chief White was surprised to see them.

"We are going to celebrate the recovery of Spoon Mouth," Rod Jimerson announced, "and we've come to claim our tribal property."

"You can't—at least not now."

"Why not?" Rod asked.

"Because we need it as evidence in the trial of the Rideaus," the chief replied.

The Senecas looked at one another, then huddled in whispered conversation. Finally Rod spoke up. "We'll keep Spoon Mouth in our Council Offices, Chief. Any time you want to use the relic as evidence, we'll bring it to court."

"Can't do that," the officer said bluntly. "Rules are rules."

A glimmer came into Rod Jimerson's eyes. "Perhaps you're right," he said slowly. "By the way, Chief, I haven't had a look at Spoon Mouth yet. It might have been damaged. Will you at least show it to me?"

"Of course," White replied. He walked to a safe in his office and returned holding the gold relic in both hands.

With a lightning fast movement, Rod took the relic from the officer. The sudden move jerked it from his clutched hands. It flew into the air, landed on the floor, *and broke into a hundred pieces!*

With mixed looks of consternation and disbelief the boys, the Indians, and the law officers stared at the fragments.

"That's not Spoon Mouth!" Paul Jimerson thundered. "It was a fake! A cast!" He bent down to scoop up some of the pieces.

The chief looked embarrassed. "I'm sorry," he said. "I thought we had the real thing!"

"What'd I tell you?" Chet said triumphantly. "The Rideaus are not guilty. Somebody planted the fake Spoon Mouth in their house!"

"I can see it all now," the chief said. "Whoever stole the Rideaus' collection did this to stall for time."

Joe could keep quiet no longer. "And I think I know who it was—the professors!"

"Careful, Joe," Frank warned. "Don't accuse anyone without concrete evidence!"

The police chief said that no charges would be preferred against the Rideaus. "I suggest we go out immediately and tell them they have been exonerated."

"That's fine," Frank agreed. "But they're still stone-broke. We simply have to find the doctor's coins!"

The Senecas offered to join the Hardys and Chet in a search for the loot. They all drove to the Rideaus' place. Joe rode with the police chief and filled him in on their discovery of the root cellar and their suspicions of the professors.

When the Rideaus were told what had happened, they stared at each other in relief. But it took a while for the good news to sink in.

Finally Mrs. Rideau smiled wanly and said, "I told you so. The doctor and I wouldn't steal anything!" Then she burst into tears.

The Hardys and Chet led the police and the Indians in a search of the barn. Frank and Joe dropped down into the pit and surveyed every inch of the dank walls, while the Senecas scoured the outside. They were still looking for an opening when Paul Jimerson ran into the barn, poked his head down into the root cellar, and said, "We found a loose boulder outside behind the barn. It leads to a tunnel!"

Just then Frank and Joe heard thumping beneath their feet. Using their hands, they quickly scraped aside some dirt, found a ring in a wooden trap door, and pulled it up.

About five feet below them crouched Rod Jimerson and two other Senecas. They had gone into the tunnel, which connected the root cellar to the outside!

"That's how the thieves got out with the loot!" Rod declared.

"What do you mean?" Joe asked. "There wasn't any loot in here, so far as we could see."

"It was stored in the tunnel. Look at this!" Rod held up a roll of coins in his right hand.

CHAPTER XIX

Lendo's Dilemma

"So the profs hid the coins in the tunnel. Probably they waited until after dark, when nobody was here but the Rideaus, then drove their rented truck around to the back of the barn and loaded up!" Joe concluded.

"Moving out gave them a good excuse for hiring the truck," Chet remarked.

"At the time I thought it seemed odd," said Frank, "but I assumed the profs had a lot of books and other stuff to cart off."

Frank and Joe scrambled out of the root cellar and showed their find to Chief White and his men, who were standing outside the barn. He agreed with their theory.

"It was an inside job, all right," he said. "The use of that tunnel convinces me of it!"

He went into the house, telephoned the U-Drive company, and after a short conversation with them had an alarm sent out for the truck.

Frank glanced at his watch. "I'd like to talk to the manager of that outfit personally," he said. "Maybe we'll catch him before closing time if we run over there right away."

"Good idea," the chief agreed. "Let me know if you pick up anything of interest."

Frank, Joe, and Chet said good-by to the rest of the search party and drove to the rental agency. It was located at the front of a large garage. The manager was young and cordial.

"I told Chief White all I know," he said. "Those two fellows showed me their drivers' licenses, and paid a deposit."

"Did they drop a hint as to where they were going?" Frank asked.

"No."

"Did you ask for a reference?" Joe inquired.

"I'll bet they gave that Zoar College!" Chet put in.

The manager shook his head. "Not at all. But there's one thing I forgot to mention to Chief White. Mr. Mockton gave me his company card!"

The man opened his desk drawer and pulled it out. " 'Canadian Gold Mining Company, King Louis Street, Montreal,' " he read. "Mockton said he was a sales representative."

"We've got them!" Chet exulted. "If the police cover all routes from here to Montreal, they're bound to catch those crooks!"

Frank thanked the manager and the three boys stepped outside. "Listen, Chet," said Joe, "the thieves wouldn't be so obvious and leave that card if they were really driving to Montreal."

"The address is probably a phony," Joe put in.

Chet looked crestfallen. "That's right. I guess it's not such a hot clue, after all."

"We'll pass it on to Chief White, but I have no high hopes," Frank said. "Before we go over to headquarters, let's stop at the Rideaus. Maybe Paul and Rod are still there. I want to ask them a couple of more questions about Wallace."

When they reached the doctor's home, the Indians and the police had departed. The Rideaus were in the living room, smiling and happy over the return of their dogs.

"Dr. Corey's son brought them back a little while ago," Mrs. Rideau said, fondling Tay's ears, while Boots lay at his master's feet.

"But now there aren't any coins to protect," Chet said.

Frank gave him a jab in the ribs and hissed, "I'm going to put you in for the diplomatic corps. You say the sweetest things just at the right moment!"

Chet flushed. "I didn't mean it that way," he mumbled. "Anyway, Frank and Joe will find your coins, Doctor."

The boys turned to go. "We'll be at police

headquarters for a while," Joe said, "in case someone wants to get in touch with us."

"Oh, that reminds me," Mrs. Rideau said. "You had a phone call."

"Who was it?" Frank asked.

"A man named Hadley or something like that."

"Sam Radley. Did he leave a message?"

"You're to phone him." Mrs. Rideau gave Frank a memorandum containing Sam's Bayport number.

He quickly returned the call. Radley said that he had completed his Cleveland mission and that the photos had been checked out. The professors, indeed, were swindlers.

"You can say that again," Frank said. "They just made off with a fortune in coins."

Sam whistled as Frank quickly filled him in on the latest events.

"Of course they never were professors to begin with," Sam said after Frank had finished. "They used that as a cover. They have records as long as your arm and aliases to match. But both have some college education."

"Maybe they went to Zoar!" Frank quipped.

Radley laughed. "They had their fingers in all kinds of pies, including the mail fraud gang which your father investigated!"

"How do you like that! We're helping Dad's case after all!"

"I should say!" Radley praised the boys for spotting Snedeker as a phony. "We've got his nibs in handcuffs. The Magnitude Merchandising Mart was one of his setups. Your father arrested him personally."

"What about his creepy office boy—the jerk that ran us off the road?"

"Oh, yes, the former cat burglar. He tried to tangle with your dad. It was a ten-second bout. One clout on the jaw and your friend was in dreamland."

"Dad sure was busy," Frank said. "Where is he now?"

"Flew to Montreal in an effort to round up another branch of the fraud outfit."

"The Canadian Gold Mining Company?"

"How did you know?" Radley blurted.

Frank told him about the business-card clue and mentioned the address of the company.

"Great!" Sam exulted. "Your father overheard one of the prisoners mention the name, but he refused to give the address. Naturally it's not listed anywhere." He added that Mr. Hardy was to call him soon. "I'll give him this info," he concluded.

After hanging up, Frank called Chief White and reported the news. The officer thanked him for the Montreal lead. "I don't put much stock in it, though," he added. "If they really intend to go to Montreal, they'll probably change transportation and abandon the truck."

"I know," Frank said.

"We'll alert the various police departments on the route from Hawk Head to Montreal," Chief White added. "Just in case."

Next, Joe put in a call to Mrs. Jimerson. He was told that her sons were not in, but that they planned to be at the Rideaus' later that evening.

"Okay, we'll talk to them, then," Joe said.

The doctor's wife insisted that the Hardys and Chet have dinner. When they had eaten, the three boys sat on the porch awaiting their Seneca friends.

Soon Rod and Paul drove up. They were followed by three other cars. A delegation of Indians stepped out and walked quietly up to the house. The Hardys were surprised to see Lendo Wallace among them. He was limping.

They all went into the living room, and the Hardys wondered what would happen. The doctor and his wife sat on the sofa with the dogs at their feet. Tay and Boots growled menacingly.

"May I ask what brings you here?" Mrs. Rideau questioned the Senecas after silencing the dogs.

Rod Jimerson spoke up. They had come as friends, he said, and wanted to apologize. "We should never have believed the rumor about your stealing Spoon Mouth. Now we know all the facts."

Paul said the Indians realized that the Rideaus had been framed. "Please forgive us."

Frank and Joe could hardly restrain themselves from asking questions. But they waited politely until Dr. Rideau replied, "My wife and I accept your apologies. And we were wrong for being suspicious of you Senecas, too."

Rod nodded. "Now that we're all friends, I think Frank and Joe have some questions."

"Do we!" Joe burst out. "What about those facts you mentioned?"

Rod and his brother chuckled and Paul said, "Without you they might have never come to light. Wouldn't you say so, Lendo?"

Wallace nodded. He looked more contrite than ill. He started to speak, first looking at the floor, then bringing his eyes to meet the boys'.

"After Spoon Mouth had been stolen from the council headquarters, I was approached by Mockton. He told me that he had been designated as a go-between. Said the thieves wanted one hundred Indian masks in exchange for it."

"Why didn't you tell the police about it?" Frank asked.

Lendo said that Mockton had threatened to destroy Spoon Mouth if word of this got to the police or the other Senecas. Then he would deny everything.

"Spoon Mouth was more important to the tribe than anything else," Wallace went on. "Without our good-luck spirit I felt that our people would be doomed!" He told how he had begun to "appropriate" masks from the longhouse itself and various other Indians to "buy" Spoon Mouth. "I also made as many as I could myself," he concluded.

He fell silent and had to be prodded by Rod Jimerson. "Tell them about your attackers," Rod urged.

Lendo's story was grim. The two professors had come to his house one night for the false faces. He had asked for Spoon Mouth, but was told that it had been lost. "I wouldn't give them the masks," he said, "but they beat me and took them, anyway."

"Did they say what happened to Spoon Mouth?"

The Indian shook his head sadly.

Joe changed the subject. "You knew we were spying on you that night when one of the thieves came to see you, didn't you?"

"Yes. It was Mockton who came to my house."

"So you tried to protect us by denying you had seen us. But the next day you left a warning, trying to scare us off. Why?"

"I knew trouble was brewing. Didn't want to see you get hurt. That's the reason I carved Frank's face in the tree, too. I thought it might make you leave!"

The boys told him they appreciated his kind motives.

"But where are the false faces now?" Dr. Rideau broke in.

"Mockton and Glade probably took them along," Frank said. "There's one thing I'd like to do, though. And that is check the Zoar College property for any clues they might have accidentally left."

Since it was already dark, the Bayporters and Paul, Rod, and Wallace agreed to set out early the next day for the Zoar campus.

Frank, Joe, and Chet stayed overnight with the Rideaus and the next morning, just as they were finishing breakfast, the Senecas came to pick them up.

The procession of cars headed up the highway, and when they reached the turnoff, they proceeded down the wooded hill and around the bend to the dilapidated campus.

It looked just the same as the first time the Hardys and Chet had seen it, with one exception. Lendo Wallace was quick to detect evidence that someone had recently walked through the tall grass.

"How long ago would you say these tracks were made?" Frank asked.

"Only a few hours," Lendo replied.

"Then we all have to be pretty careful," Frank

said. "It could mean that some of the gang are still around!"

The sun was dispelling the early-morning mist and shone brightly on the flimsy buildings. The Indians searched keenly, like beagles after a rabbit, all around the area. Then everyone went into the first building.

Dust motes rose into the slanting sunlight as they poked in every drawer, searched all the closets and looked into corners, wastebaskets, and behind the blackboard.

Finally Paul hauled himself up through a trap door into the low attic.

"Anything up there?" Frank called out.

Paul sneezed from the dust, then let out a whoop of joy.

"The masks!" he yelled. "They're stacked neatly under the roof and covered with sheets of plastic material!"

In bucket-brigade fashion the Indians retrieved the false faces from their hiding place. Frank and Joe took them outside and set them in the tall grass in front of the building.

Frank shook his head. "Wow! What a caper!"

"I still don't get it," Chet mused. "No doubt those crooked professors wanted the masks for a purpose. So why'd they leave them here?"

"Maybe they had no time to take them along," Frank explained. "Since they used the Rideaus' 'crime' as an excuse to clear out, they probably didn't dare to come here and load them."

"They must have been planning to send somebody later to get them," Joe deduced.

Paul climbed down from the attic and reported that it was now empty. A quick check of the other building netted no clues, and the boys started picking up the masks to take them to the cars.

As Frank bent down, there was a noise in the underbrush. He motioned for the others to be silent.

"Somebody's in those bushes," he whispered. "We'd better—"

He was interrupted by Elmont Chidsee springing out from behind a tree. He had a wild look in his eyes and a dart gun in his right hand. In his left he flourished a mass of fused gold coins.

The real Spoon Mouth!

"Drop those masks!" he called out. "Or I'll shoot!"

CHAPTER XX

A Rebellious Youth

EVERYONE stopped short as Chidsee brandished the dart gun.

"Don't shoot!" Frank said. "You'll be sorry if you do!"

"I don't care!" Elmont shouted, his voice rising hysterically. "All my life I've been nobody, and now *I am somebody!*"

"What do you mean, you're somebody?" Frank asked. He kept his voice even, trying to talk Chidsee out of his fanatical act.

"I'll tell you," Chidsee said, with a nervous smile that flickered on and off. "I'm going to take those masks and get myself some money—money that's all mine, that I don't have to ask my uncle for. Then I'm leaving this country and get far away from that rat fink!"

The Indians began to murmur and Rod started to say something.

"Shut up!" Chidsee shouted.

Just then Chet, from the corner of his eye, picked up a movement in the distance. A man was walking up the path behind Elmont. He was wearing a light-brown suit and carrying a gold-topped cane.

"Hey, look behind you!" Chet said.

Chidsee only sneered. "You won't get away with that ruse, fat boy," he said. "I've seen too many Western movies for you to fool me!"

The approaching stranger drew closer, stopped, and surveyed the situation.

"Listen, Chidsee, there *is* someone behind you," Joe said and took a step forward.

"Get back!" Elmont cried. He waved the gun and retreated several steps.

At that point the confused stranger spoke in a thick German accent. "Am I interrupting something?"

Amazed, Elmont wheeled around. In a flash Frank and Joe leaped on him and Joe grasped the gun hand. Frank clamped a headlock. Chet, running as fast as he could, threw a rolling block. Chidsee hit the ground with a thump.

The dart gun lay in the grass, and so did Spoon Mouth. As the Senecas rushed forward to collect their heirloom, the stranger picked up the weapon.

"Good night!" Joe Hardy thought. "Is he another one of the mob?"

"Be careful with that," Frank warned. "It shoots poison darts!"

"I've heard of those," the stranger said in halting English. "But I've never seen one."

The man handed over the gun to Paul Jimerson, who asked, "Who are you? And what do you want here?"

"I am Herr Johann Lothar," the man replied, "an agent from the Nuremberg Museum." Introductions were made and the German explained he had left his car around the bend.

Elmont Chidsee, now thoroughly subdued, looked at the visitor in astonishment. "You—you were going to buy the false faces?"

"Yes."

Lothar said he had come all the way from Bavaria to collect the masks which the Magnitude Merchandising Mart had agreed to sell him.

"We sent them a large deposit," he declared, "but heard nothing more. I came here to investigate. Upon inquiring, I was told that the False Face Society was at Zoar College right now."

When informed of the gang's activities, Mr. Lothar was shocked. "Germans have a deep interest in the American Indian," he said. "Our museum already was priding itself on the Iroquois collection of false faces.

"Mr. Lothar," Rod Jimerson said, "the Senecas will not disappoint you." He promised that the tribe would make a set of masks and send them to the museum free of charge.

Mr. Lothar was overjoyed and gave Rod his card. Then, still bewildered by the scene he had witnessed, he excused himself and left.

The Hardys now turned to question Chidsee. The youth was pale and looked like a deflated balloon.

"Tell us all about it," Frank said. "You're in real trouble with that dart gun, you know. But maybe we can help you."

Chidsee put his hands over his face and his shoulders began to shudder.

"Come on now, buck up!" Joe said.

The boy pulled himself together and began to tell his story. When his parents died, his uncle had become his legal guardian. "He was mean to me," Elmont said. "Finding fault all the time. I got such an inferiority complex that I couldn't even pass exams to get into a regular college."

"So that's the reason you enrolled in Zoar," Frank said.

"What else could I do? My uncle controls this phony joint." Chidsee looked straight at Chet Morton. "You were almost suckered into the deal, too, like a lot of other fellows."

"Not quite," Joe said.

"I know," Elmont went on. "That's what made my uncle so furious with you guys. An investigation was something he couldn't take. Then, when your father started investigating the mail fraud —" He shook his head. "You don't know Uncle!"

"Well, he can't hurt you any more," Frank said. "He's in jail."

Chidsee seemed to be relieved. "He made me help Mockton and Glade keep an eye on you," he confessed.

"Did that include plugging me with the dart gun?" Frank asked.

"Yes. You and the dogs. He wanted you all out of the way."

Paul Jimerson, holding Spoon Mouth with both hands, stepped forward. "Where did you get this, Elmont?"

It turned out that Chidsee had taken the relic from the professors, who had stolen it from the Indians. He intended to cash in the gold after having a replica made.

"The imitation wasn't ready and Mockton wanted it back," Elmont said.

"We heard the conversation. It was in the motel, wasn't it?" Joe said.

Chidsee nodded. He had gone to Buffalo the next day and picked up the duplicate. When he gave it to the professors, they recognized it as a phony.

"They knew Wallace would spot it, too. That's the reason they didn't try to return it to him in exchange for the hundred masks," he said.

"Didn't they want the original from you?" Chet asked.

"Sure. But I told them I'd sold it."

"I see," Frank said. "Then they hid the fake Spoon Mouth in the Rideaus' closet, knowing that it would be found by the police."

"That's right," Chidsee replied. "Having the Rideaus under suspicion gave them an excuse and time to escape with the doctor's coins."

"You know all about that?" Chet exclaimed.

"They didn't tell me, but I found out, anyway. Listened at their door one night when they discussed their plans."

"Where did they take the loot?" Frank asked.

"There!" Chidsee pointed to a nearby field.

While Paul and Lendo stayed with the boy, the others made a rush for a neighboring meadow. Several hundred yards away three cows were munching at the lush grass.

"Wait a minute," Joe said. "Look at this!"

He pointed to the middle where a long strip of grass was a different shade of green.

"Tire tracks!" Rod stated.

"Made by an airplane's landing gear!" Frank added excitedly.

Chidsee, meanwhile, was marched over to the spot by the two Senecas.

"They had a plane and took off from here?" Frank asked him.

He nodded.

"When?" Frank snapped.

"Just before dawn. They brought me along to help load the false faces into the plane, but it turned out there wasn't enough room." Elmont grinned maliciously. "I asked them what they had in all those boxes they had loaded, and Mockton told me it was something for my uncle and none of my business. But I knew!"

"So then they took off without the masks?" Joe asked.

"Right. I was supposed to get some crates and pack them and have them shipped to Montreal, but I didn't feel like working. I was just hanging around, thinking, when you guys showed up."

"Where's the truck?" Frank wanted to know.

"Hidden behind some bushes over there." The boy pointed.

"Okay," Frank said. "We'd better alert the police fast!"

"You go on ahead. We'll bring Elmont with us," Rod suggested.

Frank, Joe, and Chet raced to the convertible. Tires kicked up pebbles and the trio were off full speed toward Hawk Head.

Frank kept the needle at the speed limit all the way into town and braked to a halt in front of police headquarters. The three rushed inside.

"Chief White!" Frank called out. The man stepped from his office, smiling broadly.

"The thieves flew to Montreal!" Joe blurted.

Chief White nodded, still smiling.

"Well, aren't you going to do something?"

"Yes," the officer replied calmly. "I'm going to give you a teletype message. It was received a few minutes ago."

He handed Frank the message. The boy read it aloud: " 'Seized coins and thieves at Canadian Gold Mining office. Fraud outfit smashed. Thanks for your help. Dad.' "

"Wow!" Joe exclaimed. "Dad must have figured they'd come by plane. And he got 'em!"

"That's why I wasn't too excited when you told me your news," Chief White said.

Just then the Jimersons arrived with Chidsee. When White heard the whole story, he looked at the youth. "You realize, of course, that I'll have to hold you here. But I think the judge'll go easy on you since you cooperated in this case."

Chidsee nodded, cast a last glance at the Hardys, and was led away.

Chief White said to Frank, "Your father will arrive by plane in about an hour. Will you pick him up? I'd like to see him here and then we'll talk further."

"Sure thing."

The boys left, and two hours later were settled in the chief's office again with Mr. Hardy.

"Where are Mockton and Glade, Dad?" Frank asked.

"In the Montreal prison. But they'll be brought

here for trial. The coins are still there, too. As soon as Dr. Rideau identifies them and the trial is over, they'll be returned to him."

"I already called the Rideaus and told them," Chief White put in. "They were mighty happy about it!"

"Mockton and Glade talked," Mr. Hardy went on. "They implicated Snedeker. He must have been a real tyrant. They hated him but were afraid to break away."

"Dad, how did the profs ever get involved with the Rideaus?" Joe asked.

"That's quite a story. Years ago, Mockton's family owned the Rideau house. As a little boy, Mockton often played in the tunnel under the barn. When Snedeker set up the phony college in Zoar Valley, Mockton engaged rooms for himself and Glade, out of sentimental reasons, mainly. Then he found out about the coin vault and they decided to steal Rideau's fortune."

Joe whistled. "Did they, by any chance, cause the accident the Rideaus had?"

"Right. They tinkered with the steering mechanism of the car before the Rideaus left home. If they had been killed or injured, their fortune would have been carted off piece by piece at the profs' leisure and completely unnoticed."

"Thank goodness that neat little scheme failed," Joe remarked.

"What I want to know," Frank put in, "is how

did the profs learn we were coming to visit the Rideaus?"

"Well, after you poked your noses into Snedeker's affairs in Cleveland, he had his office boy follow you all the way here."

Now Chet spoke up. "The first night in Hawk Head someone put a charming false face on my chest. Old Broken Nose. Who did that?"

"Glade. You were getting too close for comfort and he wanted to scare you off," Mr. Hardy replied. "He also dumped a bale of hay on Frank's cot another time."

Joe chuckled. "But all in vain."

Chief White shook his head. "You boys have done a marvelous job. And to think when you first came to see me I thought you were just a couple of wise guys!"

That night the long white frame house at Yellow Springs blazed with lights. Inside, rows of fantastic red and black false faces hung in their usual places on the walls, looking down on the celebration which was under way. Everyone was there and excitement was high.

"These Senecas are 'real swingers,'" Joe said with a grin.

It was all fun. Not a serious moment was to come the Hardys' way until their next adventure, *The Short-Wave Mystery*.

Rod Jimerson's voice rang out loudly over the hypnotic beat of the water drums and turtle rattles. He acted as toastmaster and congratulated the boys for their help in the case. Then he introduced Mr. Hardy to the tribe.

Frank spoke up. "There's one more question to be answered, in order to fit all the pieces of this mystery together."

"Go ahead and ask it," Rod said.

Frank turned to Lendo Wallace. "You came to Chidsee's motel room. Why?"

"I hoped to meet Mockton there. Wanted to talk him out of the mask deal." He hesitated. "I was ashamed to take more false faces from my people, even though it was in return for Spoon Mouth."

"Do not worry," an old, white-haired Seneca said. "Spoon Mouth is indeed the most treasured thing our tribe possesses and we understand what you tried to do."

Wallace looked relieved. The kind words had just given him back his dignity. He stepped outside and soon returned with three lacrosse sticks. He presented them to Frank, Joe, and Chet.

Everyone applauded, and Rod asked if there was anything else the boys desired in Seneca country.

Without hesitation Chet spoke up. "Yes. The recipe for your mother's corn soup. Frank and Joe's Aunt Gertrude would like it!"

Own the original 58 action-packed
HARDY BOYS MYSTERY STORIES®
In *hardcover* at your local bookseller OR
Call 1-800-788-6262, and start your collection today!

All books priced @ $5.99

VISIT PENGUIN PUTNAM BOOKS FOR YOUNG READERS ONLINE:
http://www.penguinputnam.com

We accept Visa, Mastercard, and American Express.
Call 1-800-788-6262

Own the original 56 thrilling
NANCY DREW MYSTERY STORIES®
In *hardcover* at your local bookseller OR
Call 1-800-788-6262, and start your collection today!

All books priced @ $5.99